A Don't Hug Me County Fair

Book and Lyrics by
Phil Olson

Music by
Paul Olson

A SAMUEL FRENCH ACTING EDITION

SAMUEL FRENCH

FOUNDED 1830

NEW YORK HOLLYWOOD LONDON TORONTO

SAMUELFRENCH.COM

ISBN 978-0-573-69628-2   Printed in U.S.A.   #29033

IMPORTANT BILLING AND CREDIT
REQUIREMENTS

All producers of *A DON'T HUG ME COUNTY FAIR must* give credit to the Author of the Play in all programs distributed in connection with performances of the Play, and in all instances in which the title of the Play appears for the purposes of advertising, publicizing or otherwise exploiting the Play and/or a production. The name of the Author *must* appear on a separate line on which no other name appears, immediately following the title and *must* appear in size of type not less than fifty percent of the size of the title type.

Billing must be substantially as follows:

A DON'T HUG ME COUNTY FAIR

Book and Lyrics by
Phil Olson

Music by
Paul Olson

A DON'T HUG ME COUNTY FAIR was first produced at the Lonny Chapman Group Repertory Theatre in Los Angeles, California, in February 2009. It was directed by Doug Engalla, the choreography was by Stan Mazin, the producers were Doug Engalla and Stefanie Ibanez, the associate producer was Laura Coker, the orchestrations and arrangements were by Wade Clark and Paul Olson, the set design and construction was by Chris Winfield, the stage manager was Leah Roop-Kharasch, the assistant stage manager was Sarah Coker, the lighting design was by Peter Strauss, the sound design was by Steven Shaw and the LCGRT President was William Arrigon. The cast, in order of appearance, was as follows:

GUNNER . . . . Tom Gibis

KANUTE . . . . Tom Lommel

CLARA . . . . Judy Heneghan

BERNICE . . . . Katherine Brunk

AARVID . . . . Brad MacDonald

TRIGGER . . . . Tom Gibis

The understudies were Phil Olson (Gunner/Trigger), Luke Adams (Kanute, Aarvid), Cheryl Games (Clara) and Melissa Soso (Bernice).

CHARACTERS

CLARA JOHNSON – Gunner's wife. Strong willed co-owner of a bar called "The Bunyan," who's been married to Gunner for a long time.

GUNNER JOHNSON – Clara's husband. Strong willed co-owner of The Bunyan. A north woods Archie Bunker.

BERNICE LUNDSTROM – Pretty, young, ex-waitress at The Bunyan. Dreams of going to Broadway.

KANUTE GUNDERSON – Oblivious, dense, harmless, full of himself business owner.

AARVID GISSELSEN – Slick, fast-talking karaoke salesman. A north woods "Music Man."

TRIGGER JOHNSON – Gunner's twin sister. A forest ranger. Doesn't get along with her brother. She desperately wants to find a man. Played by Gunner.

AUTHOR'S NOTES

I tend to follow the advice, "write what you know." *A Don't Hug Me County Fair* is my fifth play (third musical) that takes place in a small town in Minnesota. I grew up in a Scandinavian household just outside of the Twin Cities. My great grandparents on both sides of the family came over from Norway. On my dad's side they homesteaded a farm near Grand Forks, North Dakota. My mom's family ended up in Virginia, Minnesota, the iron range. My parents were actually related to each other before they were married which was somewhat disturbing to hear until I found out they were second cousins removed and not a blood relationship. Big sigh of relief.

Growing up in a Scandinavian household, I tend to write stories about the emotionally conservative nature of Scandinavians. For instance, my play, *A Nice Family Gathering* (published by Samuel French, Inc.), is a story about a man who loved his wife so much, he almost told her. I never actually heard my parents say they loved each other during the 44 years they were married. I'm sure they did love each other, they just didn't say it out loud. It was understood. And the closest we got to hugging was that awkward, arms straight out, patting each other on the shoulders kind of hug. We were strict observers of the "don't cross the bubble" rule. In the end, my stories are about how it's okay to say I love you or to hug someone. Enough said about that. The mushy talk is making me break out in a cold sweat.

A Don't Hug Me County Fair is a "prequel sequel." Although I wrote it after the original *Don't Hug Me* and after the Christmas sequel, *A Don't Hug Me Christmas Carol*, the story actually takes place after *Don't Hug Me* and before *A Don't Hug Me Christmas Carol*. It may sound confusing, but don't worry, the order of them doesn't matter. Sorry I even brought it up. All three are stand alone musicals. You don't have to see them in any particular order to fully enjoy them. With that being said, I hope everyone sees all three of them.

A Don't Hug Me County Fair was booked into seven theatres before I even finished writing it. Usually, you open in one city, play it for awhile, then if it has success you take it to another city, but because *Don't Hug Me* and *A Don't Hug Me Christmas Carol* have had such good success, theatres had a built in audience for *A Don't Hug Me County Fair*. And because the set is the same as the first two, and the cast is the same as the original, theatres that have done one of the others before have an easier time with casting and with the set. I'm fortunate to have Samuel French publish all three of them. They have been instrumental in the success of the three *Don't Hug Me* musicals. They didn't pay me to say that.

The original *Don't Hug Me* opened in 2003 in Los Angeles where it won four Artistic Director Achievement Awards including Best Original Musical and is currently playing in theatres all around the country.

The Christmas sequel, *A Don't Hug Me Christmas Carol*, opened in 2006 in Los Angeles, where it was awarded Best Musical of 2006 by ReviewPlays.com. *A Don't Hug Me Christmas Carol* is a spoof of Charles Dickens' A Christmas Carol, set in a little bar in northern Minnesota. What's really fun about spoofing *A Christmas Carol* is that most people know the story, and most of the story takes place in the dream sequence, the ghost of Christmas past, present and future. Anything can happen in a dream and it does in *A Don't Hug Me Christmas Carol*, with our Minnesota version of Scrooge, Tiny Tim and the Grim Reaper.

Leon Embry, President of Samuel French, suggested that I write a summer version of the *Don't Hug Me* series for the summer stock theatres. It was on Leon's suggestion that I wrote *A Don't Hug Me County Fair* which opened in Los Angeles in February of 2009 to critical acclaim. Thanks, Leon.

The story takes place during the county fair in Bunyan Bay, Minnesota, the biggest thing that's happened since the winter carnival snowplow parade. This year the Bunyan County Fair means one thing to Gunner and Clara Johnson, owners of a little bar called The Bunyan; The Miss Walleye Queen Competition. Bernice, the pretty waitress, sees this as her big chance to win Miss Walleye Queen, to be discovered, and more important, to have her face carved in butter at the State Fair. The trouble begins when Gunner's wife, Clara, decides she also wants to win Miss Walleye Queen, and when Gunner's estranged twin sister, Trigger, shows up to try to win the beauty pageant, things get real ugly.

I wrote *Don't Hug Me, A Don't Hug Me Christmas Carol* and *A Don't Hug Me County Fair* with my brother, Paul. I wrote the book and lyrics and my brother wrote the music. Paul is the Chief of Nephrology (kidneys) at the Allina Medical Center in Minnesota, and I live in Los Angeles. Because of the distance, Paul would write the music first, then email me a computer file of the lead sheets. I would then download the music file and write the lyrics to the music. Some people write the lyrics first, then the music. It works best for us to do it the other way.

Many thanks to Samuel French, Inc. for all their support!

For more information about *A Don't Hug Me County Fair* and to see production photos, and song and video clips from the world premiere, please visit www.adonthugmecountyfair.com.

– *Phil Olson*
2009

MUSICAL NUMBERS

ACT I SCENE 1:
> The Bunyan, a little bar in northern Minnesota, on the first day of the Bunyan County Fair.

"If I Just Get His Attention" . . . . Clara

"If I Could Win Miss Walleye Queen" . . . . Bernice, Clara

"Who's Better Catching Fish" . . . . .Ensemble

"We Have Got a Little Problem". . . . . Aarvid

"Bunyan County has the Best Fair". . . . . Bernice

"I'm Just a Pretty Forest Ranger" . . . . .Trigger

"When Ya Need to Share Your Feelings, Get a Card". . . . . Gunner

"I'm the Man You'll Marry". . . . . .Aarvid, Bernice, Kanute

"What Did Gunner Do?" . . . . Aarvid, Bernice, Clara, Kanute

ACT II SCENE 1:
> The next day. The day of the Miss Walleye Queen Competition and the fishing contest.

"How am I Supposed to Win Miss Walleye Queen" . . . . . Bernice, Clara,
Gunner, Kanute

"Here Come the Walleye Queens". . . . . Aarvid

"My Campfire is Burnin' for You". . . . . .Kanute, Trigger

"Pontoon Ladies". . . . . .Ensemble

"Take Us Out" . . . . .Bernice, Clara, Trigger

"I'm a Bunyan Woman". . . . . Bernice

"Bunyan Bay" . . . . Clara

"I Lll-urv Her" . . . . Gunner

"Our Butter Face Queen" . . . . Kanute, Aarvid

"If I Could Win Miss Walleye Queen" (Reprise) . . . . .Ensemble

ACT 1

Scene One

(The play takes place in Bunyan Bay, a small town in northern Minnesota. It's summer, and it's unbelievably hot outside. The set is a local bar, "The Bunyan," complete with stuffed fish, deer heads, and Leinenkugel, Grain Belt, and Schlitz Beer signs. Another sign reads, "Bunyan County Fair Fishing Contest – Grand Prize $500 – Register Here." There's a small bar with three bar stools, a table stage right and another table stage left with 2 chairs at each table. On a wall near the door is a framed photo of a younger **CLARA** *wearing a parka and a tiara. Behind the bar are liquor bottles and sports trophies. On the bar is a telephone and some fishing magazines. In the corner, is a large karaoke machine.)*

(Lights up on **GUNNER** *and* **KANUTE** *playing cards.* **GUNNER** *is behind the bar,* **KANUTE** *is sitting on a bar stool in front of the bar. Both of them have their shirts off.* **GUNNER** *is fanning himself with a fly swatter.* **CLARA** *quickly enters the bar with some groceries, swatting mosquitoes, and closes the door behind her.)*

CLARA. *(leaning against the door, pulling on "billowing" her collar, fanning herself, not noticing the guys)* Oh, for cryin' in the sink, it's hotter than a stolen tamale out there.

KANUTE. Gin.

(He lays his cards down.)

GUNNER. Dangit!

(He throws his cards down.)

CLARA. *(looking over at the guys)* Oh, come on, guys, put your shirts on, would ya? No wonder we don't have any customers.

KANUTE. What am I?

CLARA. "Paying" customers.

(GUNNER gathers the cards to shuffle and deal again.)

GUNNER. C'mon, Clara, it's too hot in here.

CLARA. *(walking over to GUNNER)* What, is the air conditioner broken?...

(She looks behind the bar.)

...Oh, Gunner put your pants on!!

GUNNER. I'm gettin' heat rash.

CLARA. *(going into the kitchen)* That's it. I'm turnin' on the air conditioner!

GUNNER. No, don't turn it on, it's too expensive.

(GUNNER and KANUTE put their shirts on. GUNNER pulls up his pants.)

CLARA. *(coming out of the kitchen)* Gunner pinches pennies so hard, he broke Lincoln's nose.

GUNNER. Hardy, har, har.

(CLARA grabs a towel from behind the bar and goes to wipe off the tables. GUNNER shuffles the deck.)

CLARA. *(wiping off the tables)* The mosquitoes out there are as big as hummingbirds. I think they're plannin' to take over the town.

KANUTE. Not for long. Old man Hanson is gonna crop dust this afternoon with DDT, which'll kill everything in town that ain't human. We just have to hold our breath between two-thirty and three.

CLARA. I hear Bernice is back in town.

KANUTE. *(excited)* She is!?

(CLARA and GUNNER look at him. He changes, nonchalant.)

I mean, whatever.

CLARA. Love is in the air. Can ya feel it, Gunner?

(She looks over at **GUNNER***.)*

GUNNER. *(dealing the cards, not paying attention to her)* Yah, hon.

CLARA. Gunner, are ya listenin'?

GUNNER. *(ignoring her, playing cards)* Yah, hon.

CLARA. I grew a third arm.

GUNNER. *(ignoring her)* That's nice, dear.

CLARA. Gunner, do you love me?

GUNNER. *(ignoring her, studying the cards)* No, hon, I do not think your butt is too big.

(He discards.)

CLARA. Gunner?

GUNNER. Yah, hon.

(She gets right in front of him.)

CLARA. Do you love me?

GUNNER. Oh, for Pete's sake, Clara, I told ya I loved ya when we got married… If anything changes, I'll let ya know.

CLARA. *(to* **GUNNER***, sarcastic)* Wow! I am so lucky.

(Moving away from **GUNNER** *to straighten the chairs by the tables. Under her breath.)*

Just a little attention.

(The music starts.)

That's all I'm askin'. A little bit of attention.

*(***GUNNER** *and* **KANUTE** *continue to play cards.)*

(singing)

ALL MY LIFE I WANTED TO HEAR THAT I WAS LOVED.
I WAS TOLD WHEN I WAS YOUNG THAT LOVE I'M WORTHY OF.
AND NOW I'M IN THE TWILIGHT OF MY LIFE AND I CAN SEE,
I NEED TO START THE FIRE GET THE PASSION BACK IN ME.

CLARA. *(cont.)*
> IF I JUST GET HIS ATTENTION
> THINGS WILL BE ALRIGHT.
> IN MY DREAMS HE PAMPERS ME
> HE TAKES ME OUT AT NIGHT.
> HE ORDERS APPETIZERS,
> FRENCH WINE AND PERRIER
> AND WHEN DESERT IS OVER
> HE'LL LOOK AT ME AND SAY...

GUNNER. *(to* KANUTE, *holding his finger out)* Hey, pull my finger.

> *(*KANUTE *pulls his fingers. They both laugh.)*

CLARA.
> IF I JUST GET HIS ATTENTION
> THINGS WILL BE ALRIGHT.
> IF I PLAY ALL MY CARDS RIGHT
> TONIGHT WILL BE THE NIGHT.
> HE'LL TURN THE LIGHTS DOWN LOW
> AND WHISPER NOTHINGS IN MY EAR.
> I'LL LOOK AT HIM WITH BAITED BREATH,
> AND THIS IS WHAT I'LL HEAR...

GUNNER. *(rubbing his eyes)* Oh, that is rancid.

KANUTE. I kinda like it.

> *(*GUNNER *looks at* KANUTE.*)*

CLARA.
> IF I JUST GET HIS ATTENTION
> THINGS WILL BE ALRIGHT.
> I NEED THE GUY TO CLEAR HIS MIND
> FOR HIM TO SEE THE LIGHT.
> IF SOMETHIN' DOESN'T HAPPEN SOON,
> I'LL PACK MY BAGS YOU'LL SEE.
> ALL HE HAS TO DO IS HOLD MY HAND
> AND SAY TO ME...

> *(*GUNNER *heads to the bathroom, walking uncomfortably, carrying a magazine.)*

GUNNER. Excuse me. I'm goin' to the library.

CLARA.
IF I JUST GET HIS ATTENTION,
THINGS WILL BE ALRIGHT.

*(***BERNICE*** enters swatting mosquitoes.)*

BERNICE. Oh, my gosh. It is hotter than wool socks in Cairo.

CLARA. Bernice, you're back!

BERNICE. Hey, Clara.

*(***CLARA*** hugs ***BERNICE.****)*

Have the mosquitoes gotten bigger, or what? I mean, I slapped one, it slapped me back.

CLARA. Ya wanna beer?

BERNICE. Sure, it's noon somewhere.

*(***CLARA*** goes to pour a beer. ***BERNICE*** turns to ***KANUTE*** who holds his arms out to ***BERNICE*** for a hug.)*

KANUTE. Hey, Bernice.

BERNICE. *(She doesn't hug him.)* Hey, Kanute.

KANUTE. *(still holding his arms open for a hug)* So, how's my fiancé?

BERNICE. Kanute, we're not engaged anymore. Remember?

*(***BERNICE*** walks past ***KANUTE*** to the bar to get the beer from ***CLARA.****)*

KANUTE. I still got the ring, ya know, if ya change your mind.

*(taking a ring box out of his pocket, holding it out to ***BERNICE****)*

BERNICE. Ya carry it with ya?

KANUTE. Well, yah, it cost three thousand bucks.

BERNICE. Ya know, Kanute, I'll always have feelin's for ya, okay. We just want different things.

KANUTE. I know. But you'll adjust.

(holding the box to her)

*(***CLARA*** sets the beer down in front of ***BERNICE.*** ***GUNNER*** comes out of the bathroom.)*

GUNNER. Hey, Bernice.

BERNICE. Hey Gunner!

> (**BERNICE** *crosses to* **GUNNER** *with her arms out for a hug.*)

GUNNER. (**GUNNER** *holds his right fist out to* **BERNICE** *to avoid the hug.*) Not a hugger…

BERNICE. *(touching her fist to his)* …Alright.

GUNNER. So, how was it down there in the cities?

BERNICE. Oh, yah, it was awesome. I mean, singin' at the Grainbelt Lounge there in St. Paul. One step closer to American Idol, and then Broadway. In that order.

> (**KANUTE** *laughs.* **BERNICE** *shoots him a look.*)

KANUTE. *(He coughs to cover up the laugh, as if he swallowed a mosquito.)* Mosquito.

CLARA. Is that the job that Aarvid got for ya?

BERNICE. Yah. Aarvid set it up.

KANUTE. Sounds like you were real busy down there.

> *(to* **CLARA** *and* **GUNNER***)*

Too busy to send a postcard.

BERNICE. Oh, yah, I worked like six nights a week.

KANUTE. Really? That's funny cause they only have live singin' four nights a week.

BERNICE. How do *you* know?…Were ya checkin' up on me?

KANUTE. No, no. I was just lookin' out for ya, that's all, ya know, just wonderin' what ya were doin' the other nights…

> *(realizing)* You weren't workin' the pole, were ya?

> *(to* **GUNNER***)* Holy crap. She was workin' the pole.

BERNICE. "Workin' the pole," I don't even know what that means.

GUNNER. A stripper pole.

BERNICE. A stri…why would you think I would even do that, and how do you know about the pole?

KANUTE. I've been to Duluth.

(Everyone looks at him. He's busted.)

Where they told me about it.

CLARA. *(to* **GUNNER***)* How do *you* know about the pole?

GUNNER. *(nonchalant)* Oh, you know, it's just that...

(quickly changes the subject.)

Is somethin' burnin'?

(He beelines for the kitchen.)

BERNICE. If ya must know, I waitressed the other two nights, okay? Are ya happy?

CLARA. Sounds like you were doin' pretty well down there. So, what brings ya back?

BERNICE. Okay, ya ready for this? I'm gonna try out for the Bunyan County Fair Miss Walleye Queen competition.

CLARA. Get outta town!

BERNICE. I'm serious. Someone sent me an application for it, and I thought, ya know, why not?

CLARA. Really? Who sent it?

(She looks at **KANUTE** *who looks away sheepishly.)*

BERNICE. I don't know. Anyway, the winner gets to go down to the State Fair in the cities and have their face carved out of a big block of butter.

CLARA. *(envious)* Oh, I want *my* face carved out of butter.

KANUTE. "She's gotta great body, but – her face..."

(He laughs at his joke. **BERNICE** *shoots him a look.)*

Yah, okay.

BERNICE. Yah. And then ya get a chance to compete for guess what...Princess Kay of the Milky Way.

CLARA. Shut the front door!

BERNICE. Yah!

KANUTE. Yah, well, it's good to dream, anyway.

GUNNER. *(coming back into the bar)* Walleye Queen, huh?

CLARA. *(to* **GUNNER***)* I'm not through with you.

GUNNER. *(changing the subject, trying to butter her up)* Ya know, Clara was a Winter Carnival "Bunyan Queen" back in the day. Boy, she was beautiful.

CLARA. "*Was* beautiful?"

GUNNER. I'm tryin' to compliment ya, okay?

CLARA. "Back in the day?"

GUNNER. You're welcome?

BERNICE. I mean, what a great opportunity to have your face seen, even though it's in butter.

CLARA. Ya know how many people see the butter face statues? Like dozens.

BERNICE. I could get more singin' work in the cities. Put my resume under my butter face with my phone number.

KANUTE. Yah, I don't think they let ya do that.

*(The music starts. **BERNICE** looks at the karaoke machine.)*

BERNICE. Oh, hey, ya still got the karaoke machine, there. Can I?

CLARA. Go ahead.

BERNICE. *(sings)*
IF I COULD WIN MISS WALLEYE QUEEN,
I WILL TELL YOU WHAT I'D DO.
JUMP AND SHOUT,
GONNA ROCK IT OUT,
I'M GONNA GET ME A WALLEYE TATTOO.

I KNOW THAT LIFE WILL CHANGE FOR ME
IF I WIN THE CROWN WAITRESS NEVERMORE.
CRASH THE GATE I'M GONNA CELEBRATE,
I'M GONNA DANCE LIKE A FISH ON THE FLOOR.

FIRST I'LL STAND LIKE A FROZEN DEER IN THE
HEADLIGHTS,
THEN I'LL SPIN LIKE A TWISTER IN JUNE.
HANDS UP HIGH,
THEN I'LL SWING MY THIGHS,
JUST LIKE I WOULD ON A SINKIN' PONTOON.
THEN GET HAPPY FEET, LIKE A MOOSE IN HEAT,

AND FLAP MY ARMS LIKE I SAW A WILD BOAR.
THEN I'LL JUMP UP STRAIGHT, IN A GOPHER STATE,
AND SHAKE MY FINS LIKE A FISH ON THE FLOOR.

IF I COULD WIN MISS WALLEYE QUEEN
THE DOORS OPEN WIDE FOR ME.
WIN FIRST PLACE, GET A BUTTER FACE,
AN INTERVIEW ON PUBLIC TV.
I'LL SING TO SCREAMING CROWDS AT MALL OF AMERICA,
WHO COULD ASK FOR MORE?
GONNA WIN THE CROWN, WE'RE GONNA BOOGIE DOWN,
WE'RE GONNA DANCE LIKE A FISH ON THE FLOOR.

C'mon, Clara, join me!

CLARA. Okay.

(**CLARA** *joins her in the dance.*)

CLARA & BERNICE.

FIRST YA STAND LIKE A FROZEN DEER IN THE HEADLIGHTS,
THEN YA SPIN LIKE A TWISTER IN JUNE.
HANDS UP HIGH,
THEN YA SWING YOUR THIGHS,
JUST LIKE YA WOULD ON A SINKIN' PONTOON.
THEN GET HAPPY FEET, LIKE A MOOSE IN HEAT,
AND FLAP YOUR ARMS LIKE YA SAW A WILD BOAR.
THEN YA JUMP UP STRAIGHT, IN A GOPHER STATE,
AND SHAKE YOUR FINS LIKE A FISH ON THE FLOOR...
SHAKE YOUR FINS!

AARVID. *(from outside the bar)* Off! Get off me! Put me down! Let go! AH!

(*He quickly enters the bar swatting mosquitoes, and shuts the door behind him. He's wearing a fox hat.*)

Mosquitoes.

(*like a fast-talking used car salesman*)

Oh, for would ya look at this little bar, huh? Ya got a sweet lookin' place here, yah, ya do. Looks like a Norman Rockwell paintin' in here.

CLARA. Aarvid, you're back!

(She hugs him.)

AARVID. Hey, Clara.

KANUTE. *(sarcastic)* Oh, great, it's the karaoke salesman.

AARVID. *(to KANUTE, not amused)* Kanute.

KANUTE. *(angry)* Aarvid.

GUNNER. So, Aarvid, what's that on your head?

AARVID. *(pointing to his hat)* This? Oh, yah, I was in the cities yesterday, talkin' to a client. I told him I was comin' up here to Bunyan Bay, and he said, "Wear the fox hat."

*(**AARVID** goes to hang up his hat.)*

KANUTE. *(thinks for a few beats)* Yah, I don't get it.

AARVID. *(He turns back and looks at **BERNICE**. Lovingly, dramatic.)* Hey, Bernice.

BERNICE. *(lovingly, a little over-dramatic)* Hey, Aarvid.

AARVID. There she is. A vision to behold.

*(He crosses toward **BERNICE** with his arms out like he's going to hug her. She holds her arms out. **AARVID** walks past **BERNICE** and over to the karaoke machine. **BERNICE** is a little disappointed.)*

The LSS Five Sixty-two, featuring 82 songs written by Sven Yorgensen himself. Just say a word from a song title and it…

AARVID.	**CLARA & BERNICE.**
"starts to play, just like magic."	"starts to play, just like magic."

GUNNER. Yah, we already bought it from ya, Harold Hill. Ya can ease up on the sales pitch.

CLARA. Oh, c'mon, Gunner. Can't ya be polite?

GUNNER. What're we, Canadian?

AARVID. *(taking a small computer chip from his pocket)* I got ya an upgrade for the machine…

GUNNER. …Hold on there, Keemosabi.

AARVID. It's free, Gunner.

*(**AARVID** inserts the chip in the back of the machine.)*

CLARA. Gunner's so cheap, he stopped his watch so he could save some time.

(We hear a snare drum rim-shot coming from the kara-oke machine.)

Oh, it's a rim-shot.

BERNICE. Oh, let me try it. Gunner's so cheap, he gave a nickel to the March of Dimes.

(We hear another rim-shot from the machine.)

KANUTE. He won't even tip a canoe.

(We hear another rim-shot from the machine.)

GUNNER. Oh, that's great. Just great. Anyone else wanna try? Apparently, it's open mic night.

AARVID. *(off* **GUNNER***'s comment)* Ya know what, I am not sensing the love in this bar that I witnessed when I was last here…

GUNNER. *(re: the karaoke machine)* …When ya sold us that piece of…

CLARA. …Gunner.

AARVID. That's right. And it's a good thing I'm back, to give ya a little refresher course.

CLARA. *(excited)*	**GUNNER.** *(sarcastic)*
Oh, good!	Oh, great.

AARVID. I mean, ya bought it to bring more love back into your lives, now, didn't ya?…

(fast talking, almost talking over them)

CLARA. *(excited)*	**GUNNER.** *(groans)*
…Yah!…	…Ohh!…

AARVID. …Sure, ya did. And love is not just a one day thing, it's an every day thing, isn't it?…

CLARA	**GUNNER**
…Yah…	…No…

AARVID. …It's hard to communicate words of love every day, now, isn't it?

CLARA.	GUNNER.
...Yah!...	...No...

AARVID. ...Absolutely. And that's why ya do it in a song. Why?

(CLARA and GUNNER try to speak. He cuts them off.)

Cause it's easier. Why?

(CLARA and GUNNER begin to speak.)

Less personal. And I am sorry I haven't been here to remind you of that. Everyone wants more love in their lives, now don't they?

CLARA.	GUNNER.
Yes.	No.

AARVID. Sure, ya do.

BERNICE. I do.

AARVID. So do I.

(He looks at BERNICE affectionately for a beat, then to GUNNER.)

Ya just need a little reminder to get back on track, that's all. Let's begin. Ya look good, there, Gunner, give me a hug.

(He crosses to hug GUNNER.)

GUNNER. *(before AARVID hugs him)* Yah, that is not gonna happen.

(AARVID pulls back from the hug.)

KANUTE. So, Aarvid, other than continuing education, what brings ya back to The Bunyan.

AARVID. I'm the MC, that's master of ceremonies, for the Miss Walleye Queen competition.

KANUTE. *(sarcastic)* Oh, great.

AARVID. So, Kanute, I hear you're sponsorin' the competition.

KANUTE. *(dismissive)* Oh, yah, I don't know. I mean, I sponsor a lot of stuff. It's hard to keep track.

AARVID. Oh, listen to Mr. Humble, here, Mr. Campin', Canoein', Fishin' guy. How many stores do ya have now?

KANUTE. Five.

(makes a guttural Star Trek "Klingon" sound)

That's five in Klingon.

GUNNER. "Klingon?"

KANUTE. Yah, I went to that Star Trek language camp in Brainerd.

(looking at BERNICE)

Always tryin' to improve myself.

AARVID. So, Kanute, they told me you were one of the judges. Said ya made it part of the deal as a sponsor. Good for you.

KANUTE. Ya know, you talk a lot.

AARVID. Yah, I know. It's my job.

(gets an idea)

Hey, ya know what, I think we should have the Walleye Queen competition right here in your bar.

GUNNER. Whoa, whoa, whoa, put the breaks on, there, Danica Patrick.

AARVID. Think about it. It'll bring in lots of customers who wanna look at the pretty ladies, and here's the kicker, we'll charge 'em a two drink minimum to watch.

GUNNER. *(thinks)* Yah, okay.

AARVID. And it says in the bylaws that we need another judge, too. And, Gunner, I know just the guy. You.

GUNNER. They have bylaws?

AARVID. *(taking a pamphlet from his pocket)* Yah, it's more like a pamphlet.

GUNNER. Yah, well, thanks and everything, but I don't think I'm really qualified, okay. I mean, it's not like I got a lot of experience, ya know, judging beauty.

CLARA. Hello?

GUNNER. *(oblivious)* What?

AARVID. All ya do is look at the sexy ladies and vote.

GUNNER. *(thinks)* Yah, okay.

KANUTE. Okay, what do ya mean by "sexy?"

AARVID. Oh, ya know, the outfits they wear can sometimes be a little, ya know…risk-way.

KANUTE. Okay, we're in America. Speak American.

AARVID. What's wrong? Ya don't wanna see the sexy ladies?

KANUTE. Okay, first of all, fella, that's dirty talk, okay. And second of all, when I sent Bernice the application, I didn't know about that part of the competition.

BERNICE. *You* sent me the application?

KANUTE. *(sheepish)* I don't know.

CLARA. *(Sees* **GUNNER***'s interest in the competition. To* **AARVID***.)* When is the deadline?

AARVID. The what?

CLARA. To enter the competition. When is the deadline?

AARVID. Today. Why?

CLARA. I'm gonna enter.

GUNNER. *(laughs)* Oh, that's funny.

CLARA. *(not laughing)* Why is that funny?

GUNNER. *(Stops laughing. Changing his tune.)* I mean, it's not funny, like "ha ha" funny, even though I laughed out loud. It's more like, ya know…Oh, come on, Clara, don't ya think you're just a little too o…

*(***CLARA*** shoots him a look.)*

o-ver qualified?

CLARA. Is that what you were gonna say?

GUNNER. I mean ya already won the Winter Carnival Bunyan Queen competition.

CLARA. That was a long time ago.

GUNNER. Well, that's my point.

CLARA. Are ya sayin' I'm old?

GUNNER. No, I'm not sayin' that.

CLARA. So I don't have talent?

GUNNER. No, see you're twistin' my words.

CLARA. Oh, so now I'm a manipulator?

KANUTE. I wish I was filmin' this.

BERNICE. Kanute!

KANUTE. Keep goin'. I'm not even here.

(cranking his arm like an old fashioned camera, pretending to be filming them)

AARVID. *(seeing the "Fishing Contest" sign in the bar, changing the subject)* So, Gunner, are you, ah…competin' in the big fishin' contest this year?

GUNNER. You betcha. Every year.

AARVID. *(looking at the sign)* Five hundred bucks first prize. Whoa!

(to GUNNER)

You've won that a couple times, there, haven't ya, big guy?

GUNNER. *(humble, awe shucks)* Yah.

KANUTE. I won the last three years.

GUNNER. Fluke.

KANUTE. It wasn't a fluke…It was a walleye.

(We hear a rim-shot from the machine.)

GUNNER. Yah, well, ya got all that fancy equipment, it's like cheatin'.

KANUTE. Hey, everyone's got the same stuff I have.

GUNNER. Ya got a satellite dish on your boat that tracks the size and location of the fish, *and* the species.

KANUTE. *(to BERNICE)* It's got the new DNA mapping software, with "spawn alert" and "bite vision." Pretty standard equipment.

GUNNER. Yah, well, I don't need no fancy space equipment to catch me a fish, okay?

KANUTE. Yah, well, ya need *somethin'*. I mean, you couldn't catch a goldfish in a pet store.

(We hear a rim-shot from the karaoke machine.)

GUNNER. Oh, yah? Well, you couldn't catch a rash at a poison ivy convention.

(He looks at the machine. We hear cricket sounds coming from it.)

Oh, come on.

AARVID. You guys sure like that fishin' there, don't ya?

GUNNER. *(Duh.)* Well, yah.

KANUTE. *(Duh.)* Yah.

(The music starts.)

AARVID. Oh, look at that. What do ya know.

(sings)

WHO'S BETTER CATCHING FISH?

GUNNER & KANUTE.

I'M BETTER CATCHING FISH.

AARVID.

WHO WILL WIN, TAKIN' HOME FIRST PRIZE?

GUNNER.

I CAN DO IT WITH MY EYES…CLOSED.

AARVID.

WHO WILL BE KING OF BUNYAN BAY?

KANUTE.

I'M ALREADY THAT, THEY SAY.

AARVID.

WE'LL FIND OUT WHO THE MAN OF THE HOUR WILL BE.

*(**AARVID** takes two fishing poles down from the wall and hands one to **KANUTE** and the other to **GUNNER**.)*

GUNNER.

I'M GONNA TAKE MY BOAT OUT, BAIT MY HOOK AND FISH.

(He casts his line out and "fishes.")

CLARA. *(dismissive)*

WHATEVER.

BERNICE. *(dismissive)*

OH BOY.

CLARA. *(dismissive)*

WHATEVER.

KANUTE. *(He casts his line out.)*

CAST MY LINE, WAIT FOR A BITE AND WISH.

BERNICE. *(dismissive)*
>WHATEVER.

CLARA. *(dismissive)*
>OH BOY.

BERNICE. *(dismissive)*
>WHATEVER.

GUNNER.
>CAST IT TO THE RIGHT.

>*(He and* **KANUTE** *both cast to the right.)*

KANUTE.
>THINK I GOT A BITE.

GUNNER.
>FIRST PLACE IN MY SIGHT.

KANUTE.
>I'M GONNA BE KING.

AARVID.
>EVERYBODY SINGIN'.

EVERYONE.
>OUT THERE ON THE LAKE,
>SKIPPIN' ACROSS THE WAKE.

GUNNER.
>GONNA FIND ME ANOTHER SPOT.

KANUTE.
>SOMEWHERE I CAN CATCH A LOT.

GUNNER.
>THEY WILL THROW ME A BIG PARADE.

>*(waving his hand like he's sitting on a float)*

KANUTE.
>I'M GONNA BE DISPLAYED.

>*(also waiving his hand)*

GUNNER & KANUTE.
>RIDIN' ON THE FIRE TRUCK,
>SITTIN' BY THE WALLEYE QUEEN.

GUNNER. *(casting his line from side to side)*
>I'M GONNA TAKE MY MAGIC WAND AND CATCH A FISH.

CLARA. *(dismissive)*
OH GOODY.

BERNICE. *(dismissive)*
A FISH.

CLARA. *(dismissive)*
OH GOODY.

GUNNER.
ALL THE OTHER FISHERMEN WILL WISH.

CLARA.
THEY'RE WOMEN.

BERNICE.
LIKE US.

CLARA.
REAL WOMEN.

GUNNER.
THAT THEY STAYED AWAY,
ON THIS HALLOWED DAY.

KANUTE.
WHEN I WALK THEIR WAY,
THEY'LL GENUFLECT ME.

AARVID. Take it away, Elvis.

GUNNER. *(imitating Elvis Presley)*
WHEN I WIN THE PRIZE THEY'LL SAY TO ME.

CLARA.
GO ELVIS.

BERNICE.
HOO RAY.

CLARA.
GO ELVIS.

KANUTE.
ALL THE FOLKS IN TOWN WILL WORSHIP ME.

BERNICE.
THAT'S FUNNY.

CLARA.
HA HA.

BERNICE.
REAL FUNNY.

GUNNER.

THEY WILL HEAR ME SING.

KANUTE.

I'M THE BUNYAN KING.

GUNNER.

I WILL BEAT KANUTE, CAUSE HE IS A DORK.

(to the audience, like Elvis)

Thank you. Thank you very much.

(He goes back behind the bar.)

AARVID. Ya know, Gunner, it's only fair that if you're gonna compete in the fishin' contest, that Clara get to compete in the Walleye Queen competition.

GUNNER. Why is that fair?

AARVID. Cause…

(thinks) it's the law of fairness.

GUNNER. *(to CLARA.)* Why do you even wanna do this?

CLARA. Cause it's the Walleye Queen. I haven't won this one, yet.

BERNICE. The winner gets to go down to the state fair and have their face carved out of butter.

GUNNER. Yah, we got that, Bernice, thank you…Clara, it's just that…

(Thinks. A light bulb goes off.)

I'm a judge. There ya go. How can I be impartial if you're competin'?

CLARA. Well, ya can if ya vote for me.

GUNNER. Wait, a minute. Isn't it the "*Miss* Walleye Queen" competition?

CLARA. Yah, so?

GUNNER. You're married. You're not a "Miss" anymore.

CLARA. I'm plannin' for the future.

(We hear a rim-shot.)

I'll be here all week. Try the veal.

AARVID. *(looking thru the pamphlet)* It says here in the pamphlet that ya can be married and compete as long as the relationship is in a "turbulent place."

GUNNER. It doesn't say that.

AARVID. *(holding the pamphlet out to him)* Section 3, paragraph 4.

BERNICE. I'd say it's in a turbulent place.

KANUTE. Like a tornado in a mobile home park.

GUNNER. Clara, I just don't think it's a good idea that you compete in this thing, okay. I mean, you're just settin' yourself up. That's all I'm sayin'.

CLARA. *(sarcastic)* Thank you.

KANUTE. Yah, I don't think Bernice should compete either.

BERNICE. Why not?!

KANUTE. Cause I didn't know about the...

(whispers) "sexy part."

BERNICE. Yah, well, you're not competin' either, then!

CLARA. *(to GUNNER)* And neither are you.

GUNNER. *(to AARVID)* Once again, Aarvid, you bring disharmony into this bar.

(The music starts.)

AARVID. *(over the music intro)* Friends, it looks like we got a little situation here, yes, siree, Bob. And there's only one solution to a situation like this, only one, and I'm gonna tell ya all about it, right here, right now, yes, I am. So everyone just gather 'round, now. That's right, come on around here, just form a little circle, here, little half circle, take a knee, whatever, and gather 'round.

(No one "gathers 'round.")

No? Okay, no problem. Just stay where ya are, then.

(sings)
WE HAVE GOT A LITTLE PROBLEM.
WE GOTTA TALK ABOUT IT.
IT SEEMS THE MEN, HERE,
ARE BEING DIFFICULT.

CLARA & BERNICE.

DIFFICULT!

AARVID.

I KNOW THE LADIES,
THEY GET A BIG HEADACHE WHEN
GUYS MAKE THE SAME MISTAKE THEN
EXPECT A NEW RESULT.

CLARA & BERNICE.

NEW RESULT!

AARVID.

THE ANSWER'S PURE AND CLEAR
JUST LIKE AN AMBER BEER,
WE NEED TO BRING BACK ALL THE SHEEP WHO STRAY.

CLARA & BERNICE. *(to* **GUNNER** *and* **KANUTE***)*

SHEEP WHO STRAY!

AARVID.

AND WHEN THE SHEEP COME HOME,
WE'RE GONNA TILT SOME FOAM,
AND THEN WE'LL BRING BACK LOVE TO BUNYAN BAY.

CLARA & BERNICE.

BACK TO BUNYAN BAY.

(whispering) Tell us, tell us, tell us, tell us.

AARVID. I will! I'll tell ya right now. Here it comes! Any second! Hold for it…

FIRST, THE MEN WILL FACE THE LADIES,
AND THEN THE MEN WILL LISTEN.

CLARA & BERNICE	**GUNNER & KANUTE.**
LISTEN UP!	*(groaning)*
	Ohh!

AARVID.

IF YOU DON'T LISTEN,
YOU HAVEN'T GOT A PRAYER.

CLARA & BERNICE.

NOT A PRAYER!

AARVID. *(to the men)*

YOU'LL HUG AND KISS 'EM,
YOU'LL HOLD THEIR HANDS FOR HOURS,

YOU'LL BUY THEM LOTS OF FLOWERS,
YOU'LL COMPLIMENT THEIR HAIR.

CLARA & BERNICE.

COMPLIMENT THEIR HAIR!

AARVID. *(to the men)*

YOU'LL TAKE THEM OUT TO DINNER,
TELL THEM THEY LOOK THINNER,
AND MORE SUPPLE THAN A BASEBALL GLOVE

CLARA & BERNICE.

BASEBALL GLOVE.

AARVID.

AND WHEN THE NIGHT IS THRU,
BEFORE YOU BID ADIEU,
YOU WILL PROCLAIM YOUR EVERLASTING LOVE.

CLARA & BERNICE.	**GUNNER & KANUTE.**
EVERLASTING LOVE!	*(groaning)*
	Ooh!

AARVID.

IF YA DO THE THINGS I TELL YOU,
SHE'LL MORE THAN LOVE YOU,
SHE'LL SATISFY YOUR NEEDS.

GUNNER & KANUTE.	**CLARA.**
ALL OUR NEEDS?!	What?

AARVID. *(to the women)*

SHE'LL DO THE LAUNDRY,
MAKE BREAKFAST WITHOUT QUANDRY.
SHE'LL MOW THE LAWN, MAKE DINNER,
AND THEN SHE'LL CUT THE WEEDS.

GUNNER & KANUTE.	**CLARA & BERNICE.**
CUT THE WEEDS!	Wait, what?

AARVID.

AND THERE YOU HAVE IT,
WE SOLVED YOUR LITTLE PROBLEM.
THE MEN WILL LISTEN, THE WOMEN MOW THE LAWN.

GUNNER & KANUTE.

MOW THE LAWN.

AARVID. *(to the men)*

YOU'LL BUY THEM FLOWERS

(The men react.)

(to the women)

YOU'LL WASH THEIR SOCKS FOR HOURS.

(The women react.)

YOU'LL BE IN LOVE FOREVER,

TIL DEATH AND POINTS BEYOND. Big finish! Here it comes!

AND POINTS BEYOND!

(The song ends.)

Huh, huh? Problem solved, right? Right? You two gonna be okay then, lettin' each other compete?

*(**GUNNER** looks at **CLARA**. Both are very uncomfortable.)*

GUNNER. *(to **CLARA**. He can barely look at her.)* Do we, ah… have to buy flowers?

CLARA. No, we're good on that…

GUNNER. *(He gives a "thumbs up" to **AARVID**.)* …Okay, we'll do it.

AARVID. And the love is back. I can smell it.

(taking a whiff of air)

KANUTE. That's not love.

*(He points to **GUNNER**.)*

CLARA. Gunner!

GUNNER. Yah, I did it.

*(**KANUTE** lights a match and holds it toward **GUNNER**.)*

AARVID. I better go register Clara before it fades.

(As he exits the bar, he turns back.)

Ya know, that really clears the sinuses.

(He exits, swatting mosquitoes as he leaves.)

KANUTE. Bernice, I suppose you can go ahead there and be in the competition, too, then.

BERNICE. *(sarcastic)* Thank you.

KANUTE. Good luck, too, cause Clara is gonna be tough to beat.

(**BERNICE** *laughs.*)

CLARA. I'm sorry?

BERNICE. *(quickly stops laughing)* No, see, Clara, I was just laughin' cause it's funny that you're my best friend and now we're gonna be competin'.

CLARA. *(skeptical)* Uh huh…

(to **GUNNER***)*

Yah, well, I guess I'm gonna have to get some new outfits, then, if I'm gonna have any chance at all of beatin' little Miss Bernice.

BERNICE. No, Clara, see, the laugh was misinterpreted. I mean, I really look up to you, okay. You're like my mom…

CLARA. …What?

BERNICE. Oooh, I mean, older sister…

CLARA. …Huh?

BERNICE. *(groans at her gaff)* Aah.

GUNNER. Clara, I really don't think we can afford any new outfits, there, okay?

CLARA. Well, then you're just gonna have to win that there fishin' contest, then, aren't ya?

(**CLARA** *goes into the kitchen.*)

GUNNER. Yah, well, that goes without sayin'.

(following **CLARA** *into the kitchen)*

KANUTE. *(He laughs.)* Yah, right.

(following **GUNNER** *into kitchen)*

BERNICE. *(yelling to the kitchen)* Clara, it's a compliment! Ya look great for your age!

(groans) Oh!

(The phone rings. **BERNICE** *answers it.)*

The Bunyan...Oh, yah, we're located on route 22 just down the block from the county fair...The fair? Oh, yah, it's a good one. Great food. Corn on the cob, Pronto Pups, fried cheese curd. There's a new one this year, fried bacon on a stick dipped in gravy. At the booth, they have a defibyallator. Yah, so ya won't die... Oh, yah, it's the best county fair in the whole county.

(The music starts.)

Hold on a second, there. I gotta go sing.

(She puts the phone down so the person on the other end can hear her sing. To the phone.)

Can ya hear me?

(sings)

BUNYAN COUNTY HAS THE BEST FAIR.
BEST FAIR IN THE LAND.
YOU CAN EAT FRIED APPLE PIE THERE,

*(***CLARA*** *enters from the kitchen a la Vanna White with a piece of pie [a photo of one] glued to a stick. She then goes into the bathroom.)*

ON A STICK HELD IN YOUR HAND.

*(***KANUTE*** *comes out of the bathroom holding a cut-out of a train. He walks around the bar "riding" the train.)*

THEY GOT A CHOO CHOO TRAIN THAT GOES THRU THE WOODS.

*(***GUNNER*** *enters from the kitchen, and hits ***KANUTE*** with a big branch from a pine tree. He then goes into the bathroom.)*

KANUTE. Hey!

BERNICE.
WATCH THE ANTELOPE PLAY.

*(***CLARA*** *enters from the bathroom, holding up a photo of an antelope on a stick, then goes into the kitchen.)*

YA THEN GO TO THE FARM AND THEN THRU THE BARN
WHERE THEY MILK THE COWS EVERY DAY.

(**GUNNER** *enters from the bathroom, holding up a photo of a cow on a stick. He then goes into the kitchen.*)

WAVE AND SMILE, AS THE FARMERS PITCH HAY.

(**CLARA** *enters from the kitchen and throws hay in* **KANUTE***'s face. She goes into the bathroom.*)

KANUTE. Hey!

BERNICE.

THEY HAVE A ROLLER COASTER

(**KANUTE** *flips the train around. On the other side is a roller coaster. He now "rides" the roller coaster.*)

THEY CALL MEDULLA TOASTER,
BECAUSE IT SCRAMBLES YOUR BRAINS.
IT GOES A HUNDRED AND TEN
AND EVEN FASTER MY FRIEND, IN RAIN.

(**GUNNER** *enters from the kitchen, and spritzes* **KANUTE** *with the water bottle. He then goes into the bathroom.*)

THEY HAVE A TUNNEL OF LIKE

(**KANUTE** *stands close to* **BERNICE.***)*

BUT NOT A TUNNEL OF LOVE,
BECAUSE THE WORD IS TOO STRONG.
AND IF YOU LIKE HER A LOT,
HOLD HANDS AND KISS HER BUT NOT TOO LONG.

(**KANUTE** *moves in to kiss* **BERNICE.** **BERNICE** *holds him back.*)

CHECK OUT THE GIANT WALLEYE

(**CLARA** *enters from the bathroom, walking by with a photo of a walleye on a stick. She then goes into the kitchen.*)

IT'S ALMOST TWENTY FEET HIGH,
I THINK THAT EVERYONE SHOULD.
THE WORLD'S BIGGEST FISH
MADE OF NORWEGIAN WOOD.

(**BERNICE** *knocks on* **KANUTE***'s head four times.*)

AT NIGHT YA DANCE THE GRAND STAND,
SVEN YORGENSEN AND HIS BAND,
HE SINGS SO GOOD IT'S UNFAIR.
AND HE'S SO DARN DEBONAIR,
LADIES THROW UNDERWEAR.

(**CLARA** *comes out of the kitchen and throws several pair of ladies underwear at* **KANUTE**.)

WON'T YOU STOP BY AND SEE,
I THINK YOU'LL AGREE.
IT'S THE GREATEST SHOW.
BUNYAN BAY COUNTY FAIR!

(**CLARA** *and* **KANUTE** *exit with the props.* **BERNICE** *picks up the phone.*)

BERNICE. *(cont.) (into the phone)* Are ya still there?…Hello?…

(She hangs up the phone.)

Wrong number.

KANUTE. *(coming out of kitchen, to* **BERNICE***)* Okay, I just wanna say that even though you have not yet accepted my affection, okay, even though I feel we're close, but whatever, I'm still gonna be completely impartial in my judging of you and that includes your beauty skills, your…

(getting hot for **BERNICE**, *moving closer to her)*

Cocoa butter lips that taste like Hawaii…

(leans in to kiss her)

BERNICE. *(moving away)* …Okay, okay, thank you, Kanute. I guess this might be a good time to tell ya that I've kinda been seein' someone.

KANUTE. *(surprised)* "Seein' someone?"

BERNICE. Yah.

KANUTE. Who? Tell me. I can handle it.

BERNICE. Okay…Aarvid.

KANUTE. *(groans, in pain)* Ahhh…

(He quickly composes himself.)

I thought he was gay.

BERNICE. No, he's just a snappy dresser.

KANUTE. Well, so am I.

(thinks) Wait.

BERNICE. He just said he was gay so you wouldn't be jealous. I hope you're not mad.

KANUTE. No. Not at all. I just need a minute, here.

(KANUTE tries desperately to hold in his anger and tears. He heads toward the bathroom.)

BERNICE. It's just that he's so sweet and handsome…

(KANUTE groans, like a knife stabbed him in the back.)

…and he really encourages me to follow my dreams…

KANUTE. *(in pain)* Every word is like a dagger.

BERNICE. Are you okay?

KANUTE. *(calmly)* Yah.

(He disappears into the bathroom. From the bathroom, he cries out.)

I hate him so much!!!!

(Into the bar comes TRIGGER, Gunner's twin sister [played by GUNNER]. TRIGGER wears a long dress below the knees with a wig and glasses.)

TRIGGER. *(She takes a big whiff of air as she enters.)* Oh, I just love the smell of DDT in the morning.

(BERNICE turns to see her.)

BERNICE. Gunner?

TRIGGER. What? Oh, no, no. I'm Gunner's twin sister, Trigve.

BERNICE. "Trigve." I like that. Oh, but that's a boy's name, isn't it?

TRIGGER. Yah, they thought I was a boy until I was six.

BERNICE. Oh.

TRIGGER. But everyone just calls me Trigger. Get it? Gunner, Trigger…

(BERNICE smiles politely.)

Yah, I don't get it either.

(**KANUTE** *comes out of the bathroom.*)

KANUTE. Ya know, I was just thinkin that maybe…

(*He sees* **TRIGGER**. *Startled.*)

Holy crap!…Gunner's a transvestitute.

BERNICE. Kanute, this is Gunner's sister, Trigger.

KANUTE. Oh.

(*He looks her up and down.*)

I can see where ya get your looks from.

TRIGGER. Thank you. And look at you. You're just as cute as a monkey with a puppy.

(*She playfully touches* **KANUTE**'s *nose with her index finger.*)

Woof.

(**KANUTE** *almost throws up.* **TRIGGER** *looks toward the bar.*)

Oh, look. Beer.

(**TRIGGER** *goes to pour herself a beer.*)

KANUTE. (*to* **BERNICE**) I think I just fudged my underwear.

BERNICE. Kanute.

KANUTE. (*whispering to* **BERNICE**) I get the dry heaves just lookin' at "her."

(**BERNICE** *shoots* **KANUTE** *a look.*)

TRIGGER. (*pouring a beer. To* **KANUTE**.) Hey, I know you…

KANUTE. …I don't think so…

TRIGGER. …Yah, you own those campin', canoein', fishin' stores. I've seen your picture on them billboards.

KANUTE. Guilty as charged.

BERNICE. So what brings ya to The Bunyan, Trigger.

TRIGGER. Free beer.

BERNICE. I'm sorry?

TRIGGER. I'm competin' in the Miss Walleye Queen Competition. They put up flyers sayin' anyone who competes gets free beer.

BERNICE. They needed people that badly, huh?

*(She looks at **KANUTE**.)*

KANUTE. Well, ya gotta have some competition or it'll look rigged.

TRIGGER. *(**TRIGGER** moves to **KANUTE**.)* So, I figured, why not give it a try, huh? I mean, free beer, right? And who knows, maybe I'll find me a husband.

*(She looks seductively at **KANUTE**.)*

Bingo.

*(**KANUTE** starts to gag, puts one hand over his mouth not to throw up, and runs into the bathroom.)*

*(**CLARA** enters from the kitchen.)*

CLARA. Hey, Trigger!

TRIGGER. Oh, hey, Clara!

CLARA. Long time no see…

TRIGGER. …Come here, you.

*(**TRIGGER** quickly grabs **CLARA** and hugs her, lifting her off the ground. **CLARA** can barely breath.)*

Oh, I don't get enough of this. Oh, yah, that's the money maker.

*(She lets **CLARA** go.)*

Oh, say, you got a little soft, there. That's okay. More cushion for the pushin'.

(looking around)

Speakin' of soft, where's ol' butt head?

CLARA. Gunner? Oh, yah, he's out fishin'. Practicin' for the big contest tomorrow.

TRIGGER. Good. Cause I don't wanna see him, anyway.

CLARA. You two still not gettin' along, huh?

TRIGGER. No. Not since that whole pontoon "incident."

CLARA. You haven't talked to him since then?

TRIGGER. No. He won't even be in the same room with me.

CLARA. Oh, that's a shame. I'd like to see that.

TRIGGER. Yah, that is not gonna happen.

CLARA. Ya know, I don't think that pontoon boat woulda sunk if Gunner didn't put that gol' dang gas can so close to your lit cigar.

TRIGGER. You are preachin' to the choir, sister woman.

CLARA. *(looking at* **TRIGGER***'s shoes)* Oh, that's funny. You and Gunner wear the exact same shoes.

TRIGGER. *(sarcastic)* Oh, yah, our parents give us the same present for Christmas every year. It's hysterical…Say, you wouldn't need a beard trimmer, would ya?

(thinks, feeling her beard)

On second thought, maybe I should keep it.

*(***KANUTE*** *comes out of the bathroom wiping his mouth.)*

CLARA. *(changing the subject)* So what are ya doin' these days?

TRIGGER. Oh, yah, I'm a forest ranger. Oh, I know what you're thinkin'. What's a pretty girl like me doin' bein' a forest ranger.

KANUTE. *(thinks)* No.

BERNICE. Kanute.

(The music starts.)

TRIGGER. *(hears the music and goes to the karaoke machine)*
Oh, is this that fancy self startin' karaoke machine, there? I heard about this. It's supposed to help ya find love or somethin'. Let's see if it works.

TRIGGER. *(sings)*
I'M JUST A PRETTY FOREST RANGER,
LIPSTICK ON NOT AFRAID OF DANGER.
I'M JUST A PRETTY FOREST RANGER,
LOOKING FOR A GOOD MAN. YOU.

(She looks at **KANUTE** *who gags.)*

ONE WHO WILL TAKE ME TO A PLAY,
OR TAKE ME SHOOTING SKEET. Pull! *(pretends to fire a shotgun)*

ONE WHO WILL KISS ME EVERY DAY.
SOMEONE WHO WILL RUB MY FEET.

I'D LIKE TO FIND THE LOVE OF MINE
IN MY GEOGRAPHIC REGION.
I LIKE MY MEN LIKE NORWAY PINES,
GOOD ROOTS AND ALL NORWEGIAN.

I'M JUST A PRETTY FOREST RANGER,
FRIEND TO ALL, NOT TO ONE A STRANGER.
I'M JUST A PRETTY FOREST RANGER
HUNTING FOR ANY MAN. Bam!

ONE WHO WILL SWIM WITH ME AT NIGHT
WHILE WEARING JUST A SMILE.
ONE WHO WILL HOLD AND HUG ME TIGHT,
SOMEONE WHO IS REAL FERTILE.

I'M JUST A PRETTY FOREST RANGER,
NOT A COP OR A TEXAS RANGER.
I'M JUST A PRETTY FOREST RANGER.
THINK I FOUND ME A MAN. Jackpot!

*(She pulls **KANUTE** close to her.)*

*(**KANUTE** looks very nervous. **AARVID** enters.)*

AARVID. Okay, ladies, why don't we go over the rules for the…

*(**TRIGGER** turns to **AARVID**.)*

Holy crap!…Don't ask, don't tell.

CLARA. Aarvid, this is Gunner's sister, Trigger.

AARVID. *(quickly changing his tune)* And what a lovely "woman" you are.

TRIGGER. *(flirting with **AARVID**)* Oh, my, what a charmer. Looks like Christmas came early. Ya want some chestnuts?

KANUTE. Don't get too excited. Aarvid's already spoken for.

TRIGGER. Oh, poop.

AARVID. *(to **BERNICE**)* You told him.

*(**BERNICE** nods.)*

CLARA. Okay, what's goin' on, here? What did I miss?

KANUTE. Aarvid and Bernice are dating.

CLARA. Oh, well, that's nice.

> *(to* **AARVID***)*

I thought you were gay.

AARVID. No, I just like sushi.

TRIGGER. *(to* **KANUTE***)* What about *you,* hot stuff? Are *you* seein' anyone, ya big meat wagon?

> *(She makes a "bullwhip" sound.)*

Giddy-up.

> *(***KANUTE** *puts his hand over his mouth, and runs into the bathroom again. Looking at his butt.)*

He looks good runnin' away. And I've seen a lot of men runnin' away.

AARVID. Okay, why don't we go over the rules for the Walleye Queen competition.

CLARA. Shouldn't we wait for the other contestants?

AARVID. It's just you three.

CLARA. Just…us three?

AARVID. Yah.

BERNICE. That's okay. Less competitors.

> *(She smiles. To herself.)*

Butter face.

AARVID. Alright, so the Walleye Queen competition consists of the following events; talent, evening gown, bait the hook, skeet shooting, seed slash vegetable art, guess the fried food on a stick, pontoon wear, taxidermy, and of course, the final question.

TRIGGER. There's a question? No one said anything about a question.

AARVID. Yah, ya know, just the usual thing, "If you could have any wish what would it be?" kinda question.

TRIGGER. Is that my question?

AARVID. No, that was just an example.

TRIGGER. Can it be my question?

AARVID. No.

(*KANUTE comes out of the bathroom.*)

TRIGGER. How 'bout if I give ya a sexy back rub?…Like they do in Sweden with the elbows and the meatballs.

(*Motions like she's rubbing his back.* **KANUTE** *turns around and goes back into the bathroom.*)

AARVID. Still no…Oh, I almost forgot. They're gonna broadcast the competition at the beer garden, down at the fair grounds. The whole town will be watchin'.

CLARA. (*concerned*) The whole town?

BERNICE. That's awesome!

TRIGGER. (*She lights up.*) All the mens!?

CLARA. Wait a minute. Gunner isn't gonna go for that.

AARVID. Why not?

CLARA. He agreed to do it here for the two drink minimum. People won't come in if they can watch it at the beer garden.

AARVID. Well, I suppose we could do it somewhere else.

CLARA. Oh, no, no, no, no, no, we're gonna do it right here, okay. The advertisin' will be good for the bar…

(*She thinks.*)

Okay, here's the deal. Tell the beer garden that we'll broadcast it from here, but we want 25 percent of their beer sales during the broadcast.

AARVID. Twenty-five percent? They'll never go for that.

CLARA. Well, then, I won't compete. And neither will Bernice, will ya?

BERNICE. What?

CLARA. Will ya?

BERNICE. What?

(*KANUTE comes out of the bathroom.*)

TRIGGER. I'll compete. I have a new thong I wanna try.

*(**KANUTE** turns around and goes back into the bathroom.)*

CLARA. But Bernice won't. Will ya, "best friend."

BERNICE. *(After a beat, she reluctantly gives in.)* Okay, I won't either.

AARVID. *(thinks)* Okay, I'll present it to 'em. But no promises, okay.

CLARA. They'll do it. They all wanna see Bernice in her little sexy outfits.

AARVID. Who doesn't? Okay, the pageant is tomorrow night, right after the fishin' contest. We'll announce both winners at the same time...Any questions?

*(**TRIGGER** raises her hand and waves it. **AARVID** ignores her.)*

Any questions at all.

*(**TRIGGER** waves her hand.)*

Anyone else?

*(**TRIGGER** continues to wave her hand. **AARVID** gives in. To **TRIGGER**.)*

Yes.

*(**KANUTE** comes out of the bathroom.)*

TRIGGER. *(She stands up.)* I'm not wearin' underwear. Wanna see?

*(She starts to raise her skirt. **AARVID** gags. **KANUTE** turns and runs back into the bathroom. The lights fade out.)*

AARVID. Noooooo!

*(Lights are down before she raises it all the way. Everyone leaves except **CLARA**. Lights up on **CLARA**, behind the bar, talking on the telephone.)*

CLARA. *(into the phone)* Yah, Mom, I need to come over and go through my old beauty pageant stuff...Cause I'm competin' for Miss Walleye Queen...Why does everyone laugh when I say that?...Yah, I know I'm gettin' up there, Mom. Thanks. No, I can't afford the Botox. Okay, ya know what, I'm just gonna stop by, and see what I can use…Cause Gunner will get mad if I spend too much money…Gunner. My husband…Yah, we're still married. Ya can't just wish it away, Mom… Okay, I'll see ya in a little bit, then…No, don't come over, you'll just drink all the tequila…You can watch it on TV at the beer garden. Say, do ya still have the bedazzler?…Oh, good.

(GUNNER enters. She sees him.)

I gotta go…I like you, too. Bye.

(She hangs up. To GUNNER.)

Ya catch anything?

GUNNER. *(heading behind the bar)* Nah, I'm savin' it for tomorrow.

CLARA. There ya go. Oh, your sister is in town.

GUNNER. Trigger is here?!

CLARA. Yah.

GUNNER. What in the corn palace is ol' horse face doin' here?

CLARA. She's competin' in the Walleye Queen competition.

GUNNER. Oh, for bubble sake. They'll let anything compete.

CLARA. Excuse me?

GUNNER. Not you. I didn't mean…Have you lost weight?

CLARA. Nice try.

GUNNER. I can't believe she came back…Okay, well, I can't be a judge then, alright, cause *I'm* not gonna be here when *she's* here.

CLARA. Well, *duh!*…Why don't ya just watch it at the beer garden?

GUNNER. The what?

CLARA. They're puttin' it on closed circuit tv and broadcastin' it at the fair grounds' beer garden, just down the block, there.

GUNNER. Oh, no, we are not gonna lose out on that two drink minimum deal, there, okay.

CLARA. We get 25 percent of their beer sales.

GUNNER. We what?

CLARA. We get 25 percent of the beer they sell during the competition. I guess they're expecting like 500 people or somethin'.

GUNNER. Holy crap.

CLARA. Yah, we'll make a lot more this way. Plus it's good advertisin'.

GUNNER. How'd ya ever get that deal, there, then?

CLARA. I don't know. I just…negotiated.

GUNNER. *(dismissive)* Oh…well…good.

CLARA. *(sarcastic)* Thanks. Thank you. Way to go, Clara. Good job. High five.

GUNNER. Yah, right, okay…umm…ya know, Clara, I haven't been very good about expressin' my, ahh… oh, whatcha call, ahh… feelin's, and so I wanted to say somethin' special to ya that I haven't said for awhile, if that's okay with you.

CLARA. *(excited)* Yes! Yes! Of course! Of course! Wait a minute, let me just…prepare…

(She "prepares" herself for the what he's going to say.)

Okay, go ahead.

GUNNER. Okay, then.

(He takes out a card and hands it to her.)

Here ya go.

CLARA. It's…a card.

GUNNER. Yah. Open it.

*(**CLARA** opens it.)*

It says all the stuff you've been wantin' to hear from me. Printed right on it. It's "embossed," so it has more meaning. Go ahead, read it.

CLARA. *(She reads it out loud.)* "To my lifelong fishing partner. If I had a leech I would dangle it in front of your lips till you bit down, then I would reel you in like the big fat love fish you are. You are the bass to my crappie." *(pronounced "crap-pee")*

GUNNER. That's "crappie." *(pronounced "crop-pee")*

CLARA. No, this is crappy.

(She turns it over to see if there's more. There isn't.)

Ya didn't even sign it.

GUNNER. Yah, that way I can return it.

CLARA. "Return it?"

GUNNER. Yah, so I can get ya another one next year.

CLARA. *(disappointed, sarcastic)* I am overwhelmed.

GUNNER. Well, when ya care enough to send the very best.

(The music starts. He looks at the machine.)

Oh, hey, look at that.

(to the audience)

Here's a little advice for all the guys out there who have trouble expressin' their feelin's.

CLARA. *(looking around)* Who are ya talkin' to?

GUNNER. All the guys out there who have trouble expressin' their feelin's.

CLARA. Oh.

GUNNER. *(sings)*
WHEN YA NEED TO SHARE YOUR FEELINGS,
GET A CARD.
WHEN YOUR MARRIAGE NEEDS SOME HEALING,
GET A CARD.
WHEN YA WANT YOUR THOUGHTS TO BE HEARD,
CAUSE YOUR MARRIAGE NEEDS TO BE CURED,
AND YOU CANNOT SAY THE "L" WORD,
CAUSE IT'S HARD.
FIX IT WHEN IT'S MARRED,
ISN'T VERY HARD,
SAY IT WITH A CARD.

YOU HAVE LOTS OF DIFFERENT OPTIONS,
MANY CARDS YOU CAN CHOOSE.
THERE'S A CARD FOR ANY BLUNDER YOU MIGHT MAKE.
YOU FORGOT YOUR ANNIVERSARY,
BUY A CARD, YOU WON'T LOSE.
IN A MINUTE, SHE WILL THINK IT'S HER MISTAKE.

(He hands her another card. She looks at it.)

CLARA. It's all my fault. I shoulda reminded ya.

GUNNER. *(He takes out another card.)* I'm sorry I taped over our wedding video, but the Vikings were playin' the Packers.

(He hands her the card. She looks at it.)

CLARA. It could happen to anyone.

GUNNER. *(sings)*

YOU MAY WANT TO KEEP AN INVENTORY OF SEVERAL CARDS,
PLAN FOR ALL THE STUPID THINGS THAT YOU MIGHT DO.
BETTER YET, YOU SHOULD SURPRISE HER,
YOU SHOULD TAKE HER OFF GUARD.
FOR NO REASON GIVE A CARD TO HER, OR TWO.

Oh, wait, no, she'll think ya did somethin' wrong. Yah, don't do that.

YOU NO LONGER HAVE TO SAY THE WORDS SHE SO LONGS TO HEAR
WHEN YOU HAVE YOUR TRUSTY HALLMARK IN YOUR HAND.
IF SHE NEEDS AFFECTION MORE THAN SIMPLE WORDS CAN ENDEAR,
GET A CARD WITH PEOPLE KISSING IN THE SAND.

(He hands her another card.)

CLARA. *(emotional)* Oh!

GUNNER.

IF YOU ACCIDENTALLY TELL HER SHE SHOULD LOSE 30 POUNDS...

(He stops and thinks.)

Yah, you're hosed. No card is gonna bring ya back from that one. Sorry, guys. You're on your own.

WHEN YA NEED HER TO FORGIVE YOU,
GET A CARD.
WHEN YA WANT HER TO BELIEVE YOU,
GET A CARD.
WHEN SHE'S CLOSE TO SAYIN' "WE'RE THROUGH,"

AND SINCERE AFFECTION IS DUE,
AND YA WANNA SAY "I LLL YOU," *(He can't say "love.")*
BUT IT'S HARD.
FIX IT WHEN IT'S MARRED,
ISN'T VERY HARD,
SAY IT WITH A CARD.

CLARA. Yah, umm…that was a fun little dream sequence, there, but I think I can speak for all the women "out there" when I tell you that you should say it with your *pie hole*!

(She storms off into the kitchen.)

GUNNER. Oh, come on, Clara. I have a pop-up. I was savin' it for last.

(He takes out another card as he follows her into the kitchen.)

*(**BERNICE** enters followed by **KANUTE**.)*

BERNICE. Kanute, would ya please stop followin' me.

KANUTE. I can't cause, ya see, I'm a judge, and part of my responsibility is to follow ya.

BERNICE. That's not part of your responsibility.

KANUTE. I submitted an addendum to the pamphlet.

*(**AARVID** enters.)*

AARVID. Where's my little Walleye Queen? There she is.

*(**AARVID** and **BERNICE** rub noses like Eskimos, while making sappy noises.)*

BERNICE & AARVID. Mew mew mew mew mew mew mew mew mew…

KANUTE. *(separating them)* …Okay, okay, they have decency laws, here, ya know.

AARVID. *(to **BERNICE**)* Okay, get this. If ya win Miss Walleye Queen, I already have a gig booked for ya at the Holiday Inn in Nova Scotia as a warm up singer for guess who?…Sven Yorgensen!

BERNICE. Oh, my gosh. Oh, my gosh.

*(**BERNICE** hugs **AARVID**.)*

American Idol and then Broadway. In that order.

KANUTE. *(He separates them.)* Okay, ya know what. I'm gonna beat that right now, okay. Here's the deal. People come in from New York all the time to go fishin', right. I got a new line of fishin' knives that you can demonstrate at the stores, ya know, cleanin' fish, on a little stage, with a microphone. It's just like performin' on Broadway.

BERNICE. Who are you?

(The music starts.)

KANUTE. *(over the music intro)* Thanks for askin'. Cause, ya know what, I'm gonna go ahead and tell ya who I am. In song form. Seeing as how that karaoke machine conveniently started.

BERNICE. It was a rhetorical question.

KANUTE. I don't know what that is.

(sings)

I'M THE MAN YOU'LL MARRY.
MANLY MAN YOU WILL SEE.
GIVE YOU ALL THAT YOU NEED.
I GOT FIVE STORES. *(makes the Klingon sound for "five" while holding out his ring box to her)*

BERNICE.

THANK YOU, NO, TO THE RING.
WHAT I NEED IS TO SING.
YOU WANT ME TO CLEAN FISH.
GOT NEWS FOR YOU,
THAT AIN'T MY WISH.

AARVID.

HE'S THE WRONG GUY FOR YOU.
I'M YOUR MAN, I'LL BE TRUE.
I CAN HELP YOU TO SING.
MARRY ME, PLEASE.
HERE IS THE RING.

(He holds out a ring box to her.)

BERNICE. Oh, my gosh!

(round robin singing below)

KANUTE. *(sings)*

I'M THE MAN YOU'LL MARRY.

MANLY MAN YOU WILL SEE.

GIVE YOU ALL THAT YOU NEED.

I GOT FIVE STORES. *(Makes the Klingon sound for "five" while holding out his ring box to her.)*

BERNICE.

THANK YOU, NO, TO THE RING.

WHAT I NEED IS TO SING.

YOU WANT ME TO CLEAN FISH.

GOT NEWS FOR YOU,

THAT AIN'T MY WISH.

AARVID.

HE'S THE WRONG GUY FOR YOU.

I'M YOUR MAN, I'LL BE TRUE.

I CAN HELP YOU TO SING.

MARRY ME, PLEASE.

HERE IS THE RING.

(He holds out a ring box to her.)

BERNICE. Oh!

KANUTE.

MY RING'S BIGGER THAN HIS.

WHAT'S THE DEAL WITH SHOW BIZ.

I CAN MAKE YOU A STAR,

SINGIN' RIGHT HERE.

HERE IN THIS BAR.

BERNICE.

THIS MAY SEEM STRANGE TO YOU.

I HAVE DREAMS TO PURSUE.

SORRY THAT YOU FEEL HOSED.

WHAT SHOULD I DO?

HE JUST PROPOSED.

AARVID.

I THINK YOU SHOULD SAY "YES."

ALL MY LOVE I PROFESS.

DREAMS COME TRUE EVERY DAY.

FIRST WALLEYE QUEEN,

THEN TO BROADWAY.

BERNICE. Broadway!

(round robin singing below)

KANUTE.

> MY RING'S BIGGER THAN HIS.
> WHAT'S THE DEAL WITH SHOW BIZ.
> I CAN MAKE YOU A STAR,
> SINGIN' RIGHT HERE.
> HERE IN THIS BAR.

BERNICE.

> THIS MAY SEEM STRANGE TO YOU.
> I HAVE DREAMS TO PURSUE.
> SORRY THAT YOU FEEL HOSED.
> WHAT SHOULD I DO?
> HE JUST PROPOSED.

AARVID.

> I THINK YOU SHOULD SAY "YES."
> ALL MY LOVE I PROFESS.
> DREAMS COME TRUE EVERY DAY.
> FIRST WALLEYE QUEEN,
> THEN TO BROADWAY!

BERNICE.

> THEN TO BROADWAY!

KANUTE.

> THAT REALLY SUCKS.

AARVID. *(to* **BERNICE,** *holding the ring box)* Well, what do ya say?

BERNICE. Oh, my gosh, I don't know what to say. I wasn't expectin' this.

KANUTE. *(to* **AARVID***)* I'll give ya ten thousand dollars to walk away.

*(***AARVID** *thinks a little too long.)*

BERNICE. Are you actually thinkin' about it?

AARVID. What? No! No! Not at all. I love you…

(quickly, to **KANUTE***)* Ten thousand dollars?

KANUTE. Cash.

*(***AARVID** *thinks again about the money.)*

BERNICE. Hello!

AARVID. *(snapping out of it, he looks at* KANUTE*)* How dare you?!

(back to BERNICE, *torn)*

This is the woman I wanna marry. Will ya?

BERNICE. *(sarcastic)* Oh, my gosh. Ya make it so hard to say "no." Wow. Can I have a day to think about it?

KANUTE. Take a year.

BERNICE. I'm talkin' to Aarvid, ya fruit cup.

AARVID. Sure. You can tell me tomorrow. I love you.

BERNICE. *(sarcastic)* Oh, well, that's convincing.

AARVID. Excuse me. I'm just gonna go and...drink some liquid plumber.

(He heads to the bathroom.)

KANUTE. Cash.

AARVID. *(quickly turns back when he hears "cash")* Ohhh...

*(*BERNICE *shoots him a look. To* BERNICE.*)*

AARVID. *(cont.)* I love you. I love you.

(He turns back and goes into the bathroom.)

I am an idiot!

KANUTE. Bernice, honey, with all my heart I want ya to know how much I care about ya, okay, so I'll give ya fifty bucks if ya make out with me in the kitchen.

*(*BERNICE *just stares at* KANUTE, *shaking her head.* GUNNER *enters from the kitchen, and heads behind the bar.)*

GUNNER. Clara is out there buyin' outfits for the Walleye Queen competition. I'm tellin' ya, she's puttin' us in the poor house.

BERNICE. Ya won't be poor when ya win the fishin' contest.

KANUTE. *(He laughs.)* Yah, that's not what my fish whisperer says.

GUNNER. "Fish whis..." Oh, that's ridiculous.

KANUTE. I got a hundred bucks that says it ain't.

GUNNER. Yah, well, no. I'm not gonna take your money.

KANUTE. You're not afraid are ya?

(He makes clucking noises like a chicken.)

GUNNER. Would you knock it off!

KANUTE. Oh, that's right. A hundred bucks might be too rich for your blood, there. Okay, then. How 'bout a dollar? You can afford to lose a dollar, can't ya?

(He makes more chicken noises.)

One buck, one buck, one buck, buck, buck, buck, one buck...

GUNNER. ...Okay, ya know what, there, "Foster Farms," why don't we make it five hundred bucks, okay. Cause that's how much I'm gonna win in the fishin' contest. Oh, yah, it's on.

KANUTE. Oh, yah?

GUNNER. Oh, yah!

KANUTE. Well, I'll tell ya what, there, tater tots, since you're feelin' brave, I'll bet ya store number two that I win.

GUNNER. Store number two?

KANUTE. Yah. If ya win, ya can have store number two.

GUNNER. And what if *you* win?

KANUTE. *(thinks)* I get the bar.

BERNICE. Don't do it, Gunner. Don't.

KANUTE. Listen to me, Gunner. Store number two is worth ten times more than your bar, here. Think about it. You'd never have to worry about payin' bills again. You could buy any dress that Clara ever wanted.

BERNICE. *(to* KANUTE*)* What are ya doin'?

KANUTE. I'm gettin' a place for you to sing.

BERNICE. Kanute, I don't want...

KANUTE. ...Come on, Gunner, man up and do somethin' for Clara for once. She's always helpin' *you* out. I mean, have a little faith in yourself. Your sister sure doesn't. She's puttin' her money on me, nuff said.

GUNNER. She is, is she?

KANUTE. Oh, yah, she doesn't seem to have much confidence in ya, there. I mean, after ya ran your pontoon boat into that sand bar, knocking the cigar out of her hand…

GUNNER. …Okay, ya know what, she dropped the cigar before I hit the sand bar, okay! Burned up my pontoon! She is a full-tilt chuckle head!

KANUTE. I don't know. That's what she says about you.

GUNNER. Oh, yah?

KANUTE. Oh, yah.

GUNNER. *(Fuming, he thinks.)* Okay, it's a deal.

BERNICE. Oh, jeez!

KANUTE. Really?

GUNNER. Yah. I'll bet the bar.

(They shake hands.)

KANUTE. No backin' down. It's the…

GUNNER & KANUTE. Code of the Norse.

*(On that, **KANUTE** and **GUNNER** both pound their left chest twice with their right fist.)*

(reciting the oath while doing several "Code of the Norse" hand shake moves)

GUNNER & KANUTE. *(cont.)*
Hammer of Thor,
Oden's horse.
We swore an oath to the
code of the Norse!

(putting their hands on their heads like Viking horns)
Aaahoooo!

*(**CLARA** enters the bar. Everyone stops in their tracks, guilty.)*

CLARA. What's goin' on?

GUNNER. *(busted)* Nothin'. Just hangin' out.

KANUTE. Guy stuff.

BERNICE. Aarvid proposed to me, and Gunner bet the bar.

CLARA. *(re: the proposal)* Oh, that's great...

(quickly changing) What did Gunner do?

BERNICE. He bet the bar.

CLARA. I'm sorry. One more time.

(The music starts.)

GUNNER. You gotta be kiddin' me. There's a song about this?

BERNICE.
GUNNER BET THE BAR.

CLARA.
HE WHAT? HE WHAT?

BERNICE.
HE BET THE BAR, HE BET THE BAR.

CLARA & KANUTE & AARVID.
HE WHAT, WHAT, WHAT, WHAT?

*(**AARVID** enters.)*

BERNICE.
GUNNER BET KANUTE HE COULD CATCH THE BIGGEST
FISH.

AARVID.
KANUTE WILL WIN. HE GOT A

BERNICE & KANUTE & AARVID.
SATELLITE DISH.

CLARA.
ALL I WORKED FOR THE LAST TEN YEARS,
IS FADING AWAY RIGHT BEFORE MY EYEBALLS.

BERNICE.
HE CAN WIN THE BET,
DON'T YOU COUNT HIM OUT.

KANUTE.
GUNNER CATCHES FISH LIKE A

BERNICE & KANUTE & AARVID.
GIRLY SCOUT.

BERNICE.

IF HE BEATS KANUTE HE WILL WIN STORE TWO.

AARVID.

KANUTE CAN'T LOSE, HE'S GOT A

BERNICE & KANUTE & AARVID.

FISH GURU.

CLARA.

OH, YOU BEAUTIFUL BAR, YOU GREAT BIG BEAUTIFUL BAR.
HOW I'LL HATE TO LOSE YOU, HOW I'LL LEAVE MY
HUSBAND.

BERNICE.

CLARA'S REALLY MAD, TALKIN' 'BOUT A DIVORCE.

KANUTE.

HE CAN'T BACK DOWN, IT'S THE

BERNICE & KANUTE & AARVID.

CODE OF THE NORSE.

BERNICE.

WHAT'LL GUNNER DO IF HE LOSES THE BAR?

AARVID.

HE'LL FIRST CLEAN OFF THE

BERNICE & KANUTE & AARVID.

FEATHERS AND TAR.

CLARA.

I'M A BUNYAN COUNTY WOMAN, I SO WILL KILL YOU IF YOU
LOSE.

BERNICE.

GUNNER'S RESUME IS LOOKIN' PRETTY THIN.

KANUTE.

MAYBE HE CAN WORK FOR HIS SISTER,

BERNICE & KANUTE & AARVID.

THE TWIN.

BERNICE.

HE COULD GET A JOB AS A BARNYARD BREEDER.

AARVID.

AT THE DMV OR A

BERNICE & KANUTE & AARVID.

WALMART GREETER.

CLARA.

IF YOU LOSE, DON'T COME HOME, STAY AWAY, YOU TOOL.

BERNICE.

GUNNER JUST MIGHT WIN, IT IS NOT CLEAR CUT.

AARVID.

HE WILL WIN WHEN MONKEYS FLY

BERNICE & KANUTE & AARVID.

OUT MY BUTT.

BERNICE.

THIS AIN'T GONNA END IN A HAPPY WAY.

AARVID.

WITHOUT A MIRACLE, CLARA

CLARA. BERNICE & KANUTE & AARVID.

MOVES AWAY.

GUNNER. *I am so hosed!*

AARVID & KANUTE & CLARA & BERNICE. Word.

(blackout)

End of Act I

ACT II

(Everyone is Offstage.)

(There's a score board on the bar with Clara, Bernice and Trigger's names, and numbers above their names that can be flipped over when they win an event. There's a "0" under each of their names.)

(NOTE: Behind the bar are the "pre-hooked" fishing lines for the "bait the hook" competition, as well as Clara's "seed slash vegetable art," and Trigger's "Roadkill squirrel" art. These can be placed before the show starts.)

(The music starts. Lights up.)

BERNICE. *(coming out of the bathroom, singing)*
WHERE THE HECK IS MY MASCARA,
I LOOK JUST LIKE YOGI BERRA,
HOW AM I SUPPOSED TO WIN MISS WALLEYE QUEEN TODAY?

CLARA. *(coming out of the kitchen)*
I CAN'T FIT INTO MY SWIMSUIT,
MY FEET ARE AS BIG AS SKI BOOTS,
HOW AM I SUPPOSED TO WIN MISS WALLEYE QUEEN TODAY?

GUNNER. *(entering from the bathroom)*
I HAVE GOT TO CATCH THE BIGGEST FISH TODAY,
IF I DON'T WIN, I AM REALLY HOSED.

CLARA. That's right.

KANUTE. *(entering from the kitchen)*
I HAVE GOT THIS FISHING CONTEST IN THE BAG,
IF I DON'T WIN

(He laughs.)

HA, HA, HA. I'LL WIN.

BERNICE.
I HAVE GOT TO WIN, IT'S SIMPLE,
OH, MY GOSH IS THAT A PIMPLE?

*(to **KANUTE**)*

59

BERNICE. *(cont.)*

IF I WIN TODAY, I'LL KISS YOU LIKE THEY DO IN FRANCE.

CLARA.

RUN IN STOCKINGS, I AM FREAKING,

CRAP MY WATER BRA IS LEAKING.

(to **GUNNER***)*

IF YOU LOSE THE BAR I'LL SHOOT YOU RIGHT BETWEEN
THE EYES.

GUNNER.

I AM SENSING THAT YOU ARE A LITTLE MAD,

I ASSURE YOU WE WON'T LOSE THE BAR.

CLARA. Better not.

KANUTE.

FIRST I HAVE TO WIN THE CONTEST AND THE BAR,

THEN WE'LL KISS JUST LIKE THEY DO IN FRANCE.

(All four of them do the round at the same time, twice.)

BERNICE. *(sings)*

WHERE THE HECK IS MY MASCARA,

I LOOK JUST LIKE YOGI BERRA,

HOW AM I SUPPOSED TO WIN MISS WALLEYE QUEEN TODAY?

CLARA.

I CAN'T FIT INTO MY SWIMSUIT,

MY FEET ARE AS BIG AS SKI BOOTS,

HOW AM I SUPPOSED TO WIN MISS WALLEYE QUEEN TODAY?

GUNNER.

I HAVE GOT TO CATCH THE BIGGEST FISH TODAY,

IF I DON'T WIN, I AM REALLY HOSED.

KANUTE.

I HAVE GOT THIS FISHING CONTEST IN THE BAG,

IF I DON'T WIN

(He laughs.)

HA, HA, HA. I'LL WIN.

BERNICE.

I HAVE GOT TO WIN, IT'S SIMPLE,

OH, MY GOSH IS THAT A PIMPLE?

(to **KANUTE***)*

BERNICE. *(cont.)*

IF I WIN TODAY, I'LL KISS YOU LIKE THEY DO IN FRANCE.

CLARA.

RUN IN STOCKINGS, I AM FREAKING,

CRAP MY WATER BRA IS LEAKING.

(to **GUNNER***)*

IF YOU LOSE THE BAR I'LL SHOOT YOU RIGHT BETWEEN
THE EYES.

GUNNER.

I AM SENSING THAT YOU ARE A LITTLE MAD,

I ASSURE YOU WE WON'T LOSE THE BAR.

KANUTE.

FIRST I HAVE TO WIN THE CONTEST AND THE BAR,

THEN WE'LL KISS JUST LIKE THEY DO IN FRANCE.

(All four repeat the last line together.)

BERNICE.

LIKE THEY DO IN FRANCE.

CLARA.

LIKE THEY DO IN FRANCE.

GUNNER.

LIKE THEY DO IN FRANCE.

KANUTE.

LIKE THEY DO IN FRANCE.

GUNNER & CLARA. *(as the lights black out)* France?

(Black out. All exit except **AARVID** *and* **KANUTE***. Lights
up.* **AARVID** *is down stage center, wearing a light suit
with a red bow tie.* **KANUTE** *is sitting at the bar.)*

AARVID. *(holding a mic, looking out to the camera)* Are we
on? We're on. Good evening, ladies and gentlemen,
and welcome to the Bunyan County Fair Miss Walleye Queen competition. We're here at The Bunyan,
and we are broadcasting live to the fair grounds' beer
garden. Where beer grows on trees.

(He laughs.)

AARVID. *(cont.)* I wish. With me is one of the judges, Kanute Gunderson...

(KANUTE holds up a clip board.)

...owner of Kanute's Campin', Canoein' and Fishin' stores.

KANUTE. *(KANUTE has his own mic. Whispering into his mic.)* I got five stores now.

(He makes the Klingon sound.)

That's for you, Bernice.

AARVID. The other judges are myself, Gunner Johnson, Mayor Torkelson, Police Chief Bjornquist and David Hasselhoff.

KANUTE. *(impressed)* Oooh.

AARVID. Yah, he needed the work. They're watchin' from the beer garden. Hey, guys. Save one for me. Okay, I'm Aarvid Gisselsen, and I sell Lifestyle Systems...

KANUTE. *(whispers into the mic)* ...Karaoke machines...

AARVID. ...Lifestyle Systems...The fishin' contest is officially over, the results are being tallied by the accounting firm of Ole, Ole, Ole and Greenberg. There was a merger. And the winner will be announced just before we crown Miss Walleye Queen. So without further ado, let's meet our lovely contestants.

(The music starts. The ladies don't enter. **AARVID** *sings while looking around, wondering where they are.)*

(sings)

HERE ARE THREE POSSIBLE QUEENS,
WITH SO MUCH BEAUTY, TALENT AND THEY'RE MOSTLY CLEAN.
IT WILL NOT TAKE LONG TO CHOOSE A QUEEN,
CAUSE THEY'RE THE ONLY ONES THAT SHOWED UP.

CLARA. Now?

AARVID. Yes!

(CLARA enters from the kitchen.)

AARVID. *(cont.)*
> LOOK AT THEM, THEY ARE SO CUTE,
> YA WANNA KISS 'EM ALL NIGHT.

BERNICE. Now?

AARVID. Yes!

> **(BERNICE** *enters from the bathroom.)*

> LOOK AT THEM, LIKE RIPENED FRUIT,
> YA JUST WANNA SQUEEZE 'EM TIGHT.

TRIGGER. *(from outside the bar's window)* Now!

> *(She goes to try to open the front door, but it's locked.)*

AARVID. No!

> SOON WE WILL NARROW IT DOWN,
> AND THEN THE LOSERS LEAVE WITH A BIG OL' FROWN.

TRIGGER. *(coming back to the window)* The door's locked!

> *(goes to open the door again)*

AARVID.

> IT'S SUCH A BIG THRILL TO WEAR THE CROWN
> BECAUSE THE WINNER GETS FIFTY BUCKS.

TRIGGER. *(coming back to the window)* I can't get in!

> *(goes to open the door again)*

AARVID.

> WHO WILL WIN, WILL IT BE YOU?

> *(to* **BERNICE***)*

> I WISH I KNEW BUT I DON'T.

TRIGGER. *(coming back to the window)* Little help.

AARVID.

> WHO WILL WIN? DON'T HAVE A CLUE,
> BUT I THINK I KNOW WHO WON'T.

> *(looks at* **TRIGGER** *who poses)*

> SOON WE WILL CROWN A QUEEN
> AND THEN HER FACE WILL BE A BUTTER FIGURINE.

> *(From behind the bar,* **KANUTE** *lifts up a big block of butter and sets it on the bar.)*

AARVID. *(cont.)*
> SHE'LL BE THE NEW MISS WALLEYE QUEEN,
> AND THEN THE OTHER TWO WILL GO HOME.
> AND ALL THEIR HOPES AND DREAMS WILL BE CRUSHED.

(The song ends.)

Hold for applause.

(There's a knock at the door.)

Okay, let's meet the lovely ladies, shall we. But first, let's meet Trigger.

*(He opens the front door. **TRIGGER** enters.)*

TRIGGER. The door was locked.

AARVID. How did that happen?

> *(bringing **TRIGGER** down stage center)*

TRIGGER. I don't know. I couldn't get in.

AARVID. Okay, Trigger, why don't ya go ahead there and tell us a little bit about yourself.

(He holds the microphone up to her.)

TRIGGER. *(Taking the mic from him. Into the mic, looking at* **AARVID**.*)* Hello, hello, is this working? Hello, hello.

AARVID. Yes, it's working.

> *(pointing out to the camera)*

To the camera.

TRIGGER. Hello…My name is Trigger Johnson. I'm a forest ranger. I like long walks in the woods, spotted owls, and Yaeger shots. I'm single, and I can see Russia from my house.

*(**AARVID** whispers something into **TRIGGER**'s ear.)*

Oh, that's Canada?…I gotta stop shootin' at those guys.

AARVID. *(taking the mic back)* Okay.

TRIGGER. *(feeling her bra)* Uh oh, I think my bra just snapped.

> *(to **AARVID**)*

Did it?

(She holds open the top of her dress for **AARVID** *to see. He takes a look. She quickly covers up.)*

TRIGGER. *(cont.)* Ha! Got ya. Tryin' to sneak a peak. See anything? Little bit? There's a matinee. Double feature. "Twin Peaks" and "Northern Exposure." Anyway, I gotta go fix this thing. Put the Chihuahuas back in their cage.

(She heads toward the bathroom.)

Who let the dogs out…

(barking like a dog as she disappears into the bathroom)

AARVID. Okay, back to the…

(The phone on the bar rings.)

KANUTE. *(answering the phone)* The Bunyan…Oh, hey, Gunner…Trigger?…Yah, she's puttin' the rabbits back in the hutch…Hey, Gunner, when I win the bar, I'm gonna put in a frozen yogurt machine…Hello?… Hello?…

(He hangs up.)

Gunner's gonna bring in their scores from the beer garden.

AARVID. Okay…Let's go to Bernice. Ya look so nice tonight.

(He holds the mic in front of **BERNICE,** *moving close to her.)*

BERNICE. Thank you.

(into mic)

Hi. I'm Bernice Lundstrom. I'm a professional singer, and some day I'd like to perform on Broadway.

*(**CLARA** laughs.)*

Excuse me?

CLARA. Nothin'. Sometimes I just laugh cause I'm old.

BERNICE. It was a compliment.

CLARA. Yah, whatever.

*(**BERNICE** heads for the kitchen.)*

AARVID. Where are ya goin'?

BERNICE. I gotta go send out invitations to Clara's pity party.

(She goes into the kitchen.)

CLARA. Not funny.

AARVID. Cat fight.

AARVID & KANUTE. Meow.

(They laugh.)

AARVID. Okay. Let's go to **CLARA.**

(He holds the mic in front of **CLARA***.)*

*(***GUNNER** *quietly enters the bar.* **CLARA** *doesn't see him.)*

CLARA. Okay, umm, I'm Clara Johnson. I like to cook with Spam. My husband, Gunner, and I own The Bunyan, here. And, ya know, speakin' of Gunner, he bet the bar that he would win the fishin' contest today. Hope ya win, honey. Don't come home if ya don't.

(She laughs.)

GUNNER. I won't.

CLARA. *(realizing* **GUNNER***'s behind her)* Oh, jeezy beezy.

(She turns to see **GUNNER***.)*

I thought you were at the beer garden.

GUNNER. Yah, well, ya know, I just thought I'd bring in some scores in person…

(He hands a piece of paper to **AARVID***, then looks at* **CLARA***. Stoic.)*

Ya look nice.

CLARA. *(pleasantly surprised at the compliment)* Thank you.

GUNNER. *(re: her outfit)* So…how much did that cost?

CLARA. Is that why you're here? To ask how much this cost?

GUNNER. What? No. No. I don't care, cause, ya know what, I'm gonna win the fishin' contest…

CLARA. …I made it myself…

GUNNER. …I don't care…

CLARA. …Fine.

AARVID. *(uncomfortable with their arguing)* On the air.

(looking at scores)

Alright, the winner of the first event, "seed slash vegetable art," is…Clara Johnson.

*(**GUNNER** smiles. **KANUTE** lifts up Clara's art from behind the bar, and hands it to **AARVID**. There's a blue ribbon on it. **KANUTE**, then flips a "1" under Clara's name on the score board.)*

CLARA. No way! No way! Oh, my gosh! Thank you. Wow!

AARVID. What is it?

CLARA. Okay, umm, the title is "Wishful Thinking."

KANUTE. *(whispers into his mic)* "Wishful Thinking."

*(**AARVID** is slightly annoyed at **KANUTE**'s whispering.)*

CLARA. The motif is "corn on canvas."

KANUTE. *(whispering into his mic)* "Corn on canvas."

AARVID. *(to **KANUTE**)* What're ya doin'?

KANUTE. *(whispering into his mic)* Color commentary.

AARVID. I'm gonna take away your mic.

KANUTE. *(whispers into mic)* He's gonna take away my mic.

AARVID. Gimme that.

*(He takes the mic from **KANUTE**.)*

KANUTE. And there it goes.

CLARA. It's a portrait of Gunner and myself.

AARVID. Gunner's lookin' pretty thin, there.

CLARA. *(leaning into the mic)* Wishful thinking.

AARVID. *(laughs)* That's rich. And Gunner is saying, "I love you," to you. And you are…

CLARA. I'm passing out.

(We hear a rim-shot from the machine.)

Be sure to tip the waiters.

GUNNER. *(He laughs, sarcastic.)* Oh, that's funny. Oh, my gosh. A little Phyllis Diller, there. Yah, okay, well, I'm just gonna let ya get ready for the next event, there, while I go think about who I'm gonna vote for, okay?…

CLARA. …Fine!..

GUNNER. …See how that works?…

CLARA. *(disgusted, groan)* …Ahh…

GUNNER. …Cause I'm a judge. And I haven't decided, yet…

CLARA. …Yah, well, why don't ya just go, then…

GUNNER. *(as he exits)* …Yah, I am, okay. I'm goin' right now…

CLARA. …Good.

> *(**GUNNER** exits the bar. **CLARA** exits to the kitchen. **KANUTE** puts **CLARA**'s art behind the bar. **BERNICE** comes out of the kitchen, carrying a real potato with plastic eyes, nose and lips. There's a red ribbon on it.)*

AARVID. *(re: their arguing.)* Not the time or the place.

> *(into mic)*

Okay, let's look at…

BERNICE. *(grabbing **AARVID**'s mic from him)* I just wanna show everyone what real art looks like, even though it came in second.

> *(Holding the potato up to the camera. **AARVID** is nervous.)*

The motif is "potato," and it's called "You Ain't Gettin' Any."

> *(She shoots a look at **AARVID**, then to the camera, smiling.)*

Thank you.

> *(She exits to the kitchen.)*

KANUTE. *(whispering into mic)* Ouch.

AARVID. *(trying to compose himself)* Alright, let's look at a few more results, here.

(looking at paper)

AARVID. *(cont.)* Earlier, today, Trigger won the skeet shooting event hitting ten out of ten clay pigeons.

TRIGGER *(Offstage)* Yes!

AARVID. Instead of using a shotgun, she used an Uzi.

(KANUTE flips a "1" under TRIGGER's name.)

A forest ranger with an uzi. That's a picture...Bernice came in first in the "guess the fried food on a stick" event...

(We hear BERNICE giggling off stage.)

with her winning answer...

(reading from a card)

"some sort of meat and or fish or chicken." Trigger's guess was, "puppy chow."

(KANUTE flips a "1" under BERNICE's name.)

TRIGGER. *(coming out of the bathroom)* Okay, here's the deal on that one, okay. I lost my taste buds in a tragic log rolling accident when I was a child, okay... That event wasn't fair and Gunner knows it!

(looking out at the camera)

I'm watchin' you, Gunner. Don't you mess with me.

(TRIGGER points to his eyes with two fingers then to the camera a la Robert Deniro in "Meet the Parents." He then motions like he's lighting a match and setting a fire.)

That's fire. I don't know what it's burnin', but it's somethin' of yours!

AARVID. Alright, we're gonna be back in a few minutes with our pontoon wear event. So stay tuned, beer garden, ya don't wanna miss the sexy ladies. Especially Bernice, my girlfriend. And...we're out.

(as he exits)

Bernice, honey?...Lambchop?

(**AARVID** *exits to the kitchen as* **KANUTE** *despondently watches him.*)

KANUTE. Ah, crap.

TRIGGER. Oh, forget about Bernice. You deserve a real woman. I'm talkin' about a woman who can field dress a moose.

(motions like she's slicing a moose, with sound effects)

Someone who appreciates you for the manly man that you are. And successful, too.

KANUTE. *(humble)* Yah, well.

TRIGGER. Oh, look at you bein' all humble, there, Mister Campin', Canoein', Fishin' guy. How big a fish did ya catch today? Whisper it.

(She leans over for **KANUTE** *to whisper in her ear.)*

KANUTE. *(reluctant)* Oh, I don't think I really should.

TRIGGER. *(pointing to her ear)* Come on. Right here. I wanna feel your warm breath on my face.

KANUTE. That's not an incentive.

TRIGGER. Just whisper it!

(**KANUTE** *whispers something.)*

Oh, my.

(suggestive) That's bigger than I thought.

KANUTE. Oh, well, women mis-underestimate me.

TRIGGER. Well, hello, there, mister manly man…I like to troll for musky…Do you?

KANUTE. You betcha.

TRIGGER. It's hard to troll in a straight line, though, isn't it? Sometimes ya get…off course.

(suggestive)

KANUTE. *(nervous)* I think I'm a little off course right now.

TRIGGER. *(moves close to him)* Well, then let me help ya get back…on course.

(blows in his ear)

KANUTE. Are we talkin' about fishin'?

TRIGGER. Ya know, if ya really want, I can help ya get Bernice back.

KANUTE. Ya can?

TRIGGER. *(seductively)* Yah, we'll make her jealous.

KANUTE. Why would ya do that, I mean, ya know, help me?

(The music starts.)

TRIGGER. *(to the machine)* Thank you.

(to **KANUTE***)*

That's my cue.

(sings)

I DROPPED MY JAW
THE MOMENT I SAW YOU
MY HEART SKIPPED ONE BEAT OR TWO.
YOUR LOVE I'M YEARNIN'
MY CAMPFIRE IS BURNIN'
BABY, MY FLAME IS LIT FOR YOU.

I'LL BAIT YOUR HOOK,
I'LL CLEAN FISH AND COOK,
I PROMISE TO TIP YOUR CANOE.

KANUTE. Is that dirty?

TRIGGER.

MY TENT IS OPEN,
MY HEART IS HOPIN',
MAYBE, YOU FEEL THE WAY I DO.

KANUTE. I better go.

(He starts to leave. She grabs him so he doesn't.)

TRIGGER.

YOU'RE SMART AND YOUR STRONG.

KANUTE. What?

TRIGGER.

AND YOU'RE SO HANDSOME IT ISN'T FAIR.
TO YOU I BELONG.
BABY, YOU COULD MODEL UNDERWEAR.

KANUTE. Really?

(He turns back.)

TRIGGER.
YOU'RE SUCH A MAN,
BIG MUSCLES AND TAN
THE LADIES MUST ALL FALL FOR YOU.

KANUTE. *(humble)* Well…

TRIGGER.
I HOPE YOU SEE
I WANT YOU FOR ME.
PLEASE TELL ME YOU FEEL THE SAME WAY TOO.

KANUTE.
IT'S TRUE I'M A MAN AND
ALL THE LADIES WANT PART OF ME.
I'M BIG IN JAPAN.
BABY, WITH ONE LOOK I'LL SET YOU FREE.

(He shoots **TRIGGER** *an "Elvis" look.)*

TRIGGER. *(melting)* Oh!

(She quickly grabs **KANUTE**'s *hand and dances the Tango. He's nervous.)*

COME DANCE WITH ME,
TOGETHER WE'LL BE,
FOREVER TIL DEATH DO US PART.

TRIGGER & KANUTE. *(***KANUTE*** gets into it.)*
WE'LL WALK THE LAKESHORE,
SHOOT DUCKS AND HUNT BOAR,
FISH WITH A SPEAR
WHILE DRINKING A BEER
I'LL LOVE YOU MY DEAR
WITH ALL MY HEART.

(The song ends. **TRIGGER** *dips* **KANUTE**, *kissing him.* **KANUTE**, *arms flailing, struggles to get away as* **AARVID** *enters the front door and sees them kissing.* **TRIGGER** *and* **KANUTE** *look up to see* **AARVID**. *They're "busted.")*

*(The lights black out. **TRIGGER** exits. Lights up. **AARVID** is down stage center holding the microphone. **KANUTE** sits at the bar staring straight ahead, disheveled, in shock from what just happened.)*

AARVID. *(to **KANUTE**, into mic)* Kissing Trigger? Really?…

KANUTE. *(in shock)* I can't get the taste outta my mouth.

AARVID. She was workin' you like a pit bull on a jogger.

KANUTE. *(angry)* Movin' on, okay, just do the thing!

AARVID. *(to the camera)* Do you like bait? Who doesn't? And now a word from our sponsor.

KANUTE. **(KANUTE** *blows into a pitch pipe then sings into his mic, a cappella.)*
KANUTE'S BAIT MART,
KANUTE'S BAIT MART,
I GOT WORMS……DO YOU?!

*(He points to the camera. To **AARVID**.)*

I wrote that myself.

AARVID. Couldn't tell…Okay, next up is the pontoon wear event. Are the ladies ready back there?

TRIGGER & CLARA & BERNICE. *(offstage)* Now?!

AARVID. Just a second. Kanute, why don't ya go ahead, there, and start us off.

KANUTE. Thank you, Aarvid. Okey dokey, come on out, girls!

*(The music starts, and the ladies enter. First **BERNICE**, then **CLARA** then **TRIGGER**. **BERNICE** wears a sexy bikini or equivalent. **CLARA** is a little more conservatively dressed. **TRIGGER** has an old fashioned bloomer looking thing on with a life preserver around her neck, with a coconut bra over it, carrying a little beer cooler "Igloo." **KANUTE** looks at the camera. He doesn't see the ladies as they enter.)*

(Sings into mic.)

WELCOME TO THE PONTOON LADIES,
WITH THEIR PONTOON WEAR.

(**KANUTE** *looks back and sees* **BERNICE** *in her skimpy outfit. He grabs a bar towel to cover up* **BERNICE**.)

Oh, no.

(**AARVID** *takes over singing as* **KANUTE** *tries to cover up* **BERNICE**.)

AARVID.

THEY'RE THE SEXY PONTOON LADIES.

BERNICE. *(to* **KANUTE***)* Stop it.

(**BERNICE** *pushes* **KANUTE** *away. A defeated* **KANUTE** *moves stage left of* **TRIGGER**, *while* **AARVID** *is stage right of* **BERNICE**.)

AARVID.

CAN'T HELP BUT TO STARE.

I HAVE GOT MY EYE ON A SPECIAL LADY.

KANUTE.

I HAVE FOUND THE ONE.

(to **TRIGGER**, *trying to make* **BERNICE** *jealous)*

SHE'S A DAINTY, LOVELY LADY. *(looking at* **TRIGGER***)*

SHOOTS AN UZI JUST FOR FUN.

TRIGGER. *(to* **KANUTE***)* I love you.

KANUTE. *(to* **TRIGGER***)*

SHE'S MY LOVE, SHE'S MY SOUL MATE.

BERNICE. Wait, what?

KANUTE.

SHE APPRECIATES MEN WITH MONEY.

IN A BOAT SHE CAN TROLL STRAIGHT.

SHE'S ALL I NEED.

MY GIANT SWEDE.

(He gushes over **TRIGGER** *as* **AARVID** *takes over singing.* **BERNICE** *and* **CLARA** *realize* **KANUTE** *is falling for* **TRIGGER**.)

AARVID.

HERE THEY ARE THE PONTOON LADIES.

PRETTY AS A ROSE.

HERE SHE IS MY PONTOON LADY,

(to **BERNICE***)*

WEARING SKIMPY CLOTHES.

KANUTE. *(re: Bernice)*

LOOKIN' LIKE A TWIG WHO NEEDS A SANDWICH,

SHE'S TOO THIN FOR ME.

HERE'S MY GIRL AND I'M HER MANWICH.

(to **TRIGGER***)*

SHE COULD EAT MY WEIGHT IN BRIE.

*(***BERNICE** *and* **CLARA** *are in shock.)*

TRIGGER. Yummy.

AARVID. Ladies!

TRIGGER & CLARA & BERNICE. *(***CLARA** *and* **BERNICE** *quickly compose themselves.)*

WE'RE THE BUNYAN BAY WOMEN.

TURNIN' HEADS AS WE BOARD THE PONTOON.

WE ARE DRESSED TO GO SWIMMIN'.

DON'T MEAN TO GLOAT.

WE'LL FLOAT YOUR BOAT.

WE HAVE ONE FOR EVERY TASTE BUD,

TRIGGER.

SPICY,

BERNICE.

HOT,

CLARA.

AND MILD.

TRIGGER & CLARA & BERNICE.

UNLIKE FISH WE DON'T HAVE COLD BLOOD.

WE'RE THE PONTOON GIRLS GONE WILD.

BERNICE. Kanute, what's the deal with you and Trigger?

TRIGGER. Kanute and I are gettin' married!

KANUTE. We are?

CLARA. Holy crap.

TRIGGER. We're gonna have a quick wedding right after the competition.

KANUTE. We are?

TRIGGER. Yah.

(**TRIGGER** *gives* **KANUTE** *a knowing look.*)

(**AARVID** *nervously looks at the camera. They're still on the air.*)

KANUTE. *(to* **BERNICE,** *going with it)* That's right. And it's your loss, okay. So, too bad for you.

TRIGGER. Yah. And he already got the ring. I've seen it.

BERNICE. Wait a minute. That's *my* ring!

KANUTE. *(to* **BERNICE,** *surprised)* What?

TRIGGER. What?

CLARA. What?

AARVID. What?

BERNICE. Wow. Where did that come from?

AARVID. *(irritated)* Movin' on. Our next event is "bait the hook."

(*The ladies go behind the bar, first* **CLARA** *then* **BERNICE** *then* **TRIGGER.**)

In this event we're lookin' for speed, technique, and difficulty. Okay, ladies, show us the hooks you're gonna bait.

(**CLARA, TRIGGER** *and* **BERNICE** *lift up their bare hooks.*)

TRIGGER. Oh, look. Three hookers…

AARVID. …Okay.

KANUTE. *(into his mic)* Which one will be the Master Bai…

AARVID. *(cutting off* **KANUTE,** *before he can say "Baiter")* …Alrighty, then.

CLARA. Can I do it blindfolded?

AARVID. "Blindfolded?"

(**KANUTE** *puts a blindfold on her.*)

CLARA. Yah, I'd like to do it one-handed, too.

AARVID. Really?

CLARA. Yah, cause usually I don't have much time so I steer my Evenrude nine with one hand, while baitin' the hook with the other.

BERNICE. Show off.

CLARA. I can't help it, I'm old.

AARVID. Okay, everyone ready?

TRIGGER. Yah.

BERNICE. Sure.

CLARA. You betcha.

AARVID. *(looks at his watch)* Ready…and go.

(The ladies go to work on baiting the hook, below the bar. Note: They switch the "bare" hook with one that's pre-hooked behind the bar.)

(CLARA lifts her hook up by the line to show everyone. The line has a huge tackle on it with several hooks. On each hook are fake minnows, worms, and other types of bait. It's truly a work of art.)

CLARA. Done.

KANUTE. Holy crap.

BERNICE. *(lifting up her single hook with a tiny fake minnow on it)* Done.

AARVID. Oh, how cute.

TRIGGER. *(lifting up a fishing line with a stick of dynamite and an unlit fuse hanging from it)* Done.

AARVID. Good gravy, it's dynamite…Wow. Okay, very good, very good. It seems like Clara hesitated just a little bit, there, but…

CLARA. …I did?

(taking the blindfold off)

AARVID. Little bit. I've seen ya do it faster. No big deal.

(to BERNICE)

Oh, look at Bernice with her cute little minnow, there. And Trigger, the…forest ranger, has dynamite.

(KANUTE writes on his clip board.)

TRIGGER. I'm not messin' around!

AARVID. So disturbing.

(**KANUTE** *writes on his clip board.*)

KANUTE. *(cont.)* Okay, up next is our evening wear competition. Ladies if you'd like to go get ready, there.

(*He gestures to the kitchen.* **CLARA** *and* **BERNICE** *exit.*)

TRIGGER. *(to* **KANUTE,** *as she exits)* See ya soon, husband to be. Love you. I just wanted to tell ya somethin'. What was it? Oh, yah, I have nine guns.

KANUTE. *(stunned)* Okay. That's great. Wow. Oh, boy.

(**TRIGGER** *is gone. To* **AARVID.**)

Will you please kill me?

AARVID. *(to the camera)* We'll be back in a minute. And… we're out.

(*to* **KANUTE**)

Okay, explain to me what you were thinkin', there, when ya proposed to Trigger.

KANUTE. I didn't propose!

AARVID. Well, she thinks ya did.

KANUTE. I was just goin' along to make Bernice jealous so I could steal her back from you.

AARVID. You know I can hear ya, right?

KANUTE. Come on, Aarvid, I really need your help.

AARVID. You want *my* help stealin' *my* girlfriend?

KANUTE. *(thinks)* Please.

AARVID. *(groans)* Ahh…Just tell Trigger ya made a mistake and you're not ready to get married.

KANUTE. She has nine guns!…Ya know, maybe gettin' married won't be so bad.

AARVID. Yah, maybe. If she didn't have the sex appeal of Jabba the Hutt.

KANUTE. At least she compliments me.

AARVID. You would marry my grandmother if she complimented ya.

KANUTE. *(thinks)* Is she available?

AARVID. Ignoring that.

KANUTE. This is all your fault, ya know, for stealin' Bernice from me.

AARVID. Yah, well, I don't have her yet, okay, so…

(arguing, talking over each other)

KANUTE. …Well, ya proposed to her!…

AARVID. …Yah, well, so did you!…

KANUTE. …You're a home-wrecker!…

AARVID. …You're a man-child!…

KANUTE. …You wear lipstick!…

AARVID. …It's cherry sunscreen!…

KANUTE. *(looking at the camera)* …What's that red light?

AARVID. *(to the camera)* And…we're live.

(reading a piece of paper)

Be sure to stop by Kanute's Lutheran Hall of Fame where first time visitors receive a free glass of Leech Lake Merlot in the new Herring and Wafer Bar.

*(**KANUTE** blows into a pitch pipe. While **KANUTE** gives his over-dramatic sermon, **AARVID** hums Ave Maria into the mic.)*

KANUTE. *(sermon-like into mic)*

Friends, come to Kanute's Lutheran Hall of Fame
where the wine is real and the sermon is tame
and ya got no guilt cause there's no confession.
No Holy Water and no genuflectin'…
We promise not to judge you.

AARVID & KANUTE. Out loud.

AARVID. *(looking at a piece of paper)* Okay, earlier today Trigger won the taxidermy event with her "Roadkill Squirrel."

*(**KANUTE** holds up the winning "Roadkill Squirrel.")*

TRIGGER. *(offstage)* I know how to stuff it!

KANUTE. *(whispers into mic)* Fresh from Highway 10, folks. It's still warm.

(**KANUTE** *flips a "2" under* **TRIGGER**'s *name.*)

AARVID. Okay, next up is the evening gown event. Ladies, come on out!

(The music starts. The ladies enter.)

BERNICE. *(singing)*
THEY SAY YOU CAN DRESS THEM UP
BUT YA CAN'T TAKE THEM OUT.

CLARA.
WE ARE HERE TO SAY TO YOU
THAT ISN'T TRUE.

TRIGGER.
YOU CAN DRESS US UP.
AND YA SURE CAN TAKE US OUT.

CLARA & BERNICE & TRIGGER.
BUT YA CAN'T HAVE US
IF YA DON'T KNOW WHAT TO DO.

KANUTE. Is that dirty?

CLARA & BERNICE & TRIGGER.
YA JUST SMILE THEN TELL US WE'RE BEAUTIFUL
AND THEN WE'LL SAY THANK YOU.
TAKE OUR HAND AND OPEN THE DOOR
JUST LIKE THE PERFECT GENTLEMAN WE LONG FOR.

TAKE US OUT TO DINNER.
WE'LL ORDER ONE OR TWO SHRIMP COCKTAILS.
THEN IT'S OFF TO THE V-F-W
TO DANCE THE NIGHT AWAY JUST ME AND YOU.

BERNICE.
WE WILL HIT THE TOWN,

CLARA.
WE WILL CLOSE IT DOWN.

BERNICE.
WE WILL DANCE TIL DAWN,

TRIGGER.
OR UNTIL THE BEER IS GONE.

BERNICE.
    WE WILL CUT THE RUG,
CLARA.
    WE WILL KISS AND HUG.
BERNICE.
    WE WILL DANCE REAL HARD.
TRIGGER.
    WE ACCEPT ALL CREDIT CARDS.
KANUTE. Wait, what?
CLARA & BERNICE & TRIGGER.
    TAKE US OUT, WE'LL HELP PUT OUT THE FIRE.
    TAKE US OUT, ANYTHING YOU DESIRE.
    TAKE US OUT, WE'LL GIVE YA FREQUENT FLIER
    MILES WITH EVERY DATE…YEAH!
KANUTE. *(to* **BERNICE***)* Okay, so…ya take credit cards, and ya give frequent flyer miles with every date.
BERNICE. Yah. We're escorts.
KANUTE. "Escorts." I am so proud of you.
BERNICE. Thanks.
KANUTE. Sarcasm!
BERNICE. Oh.
AARVID. Okay, we're gonna go ahead and ask the final question next, then we'll finish up with the talent competition. Trigger, let's start with you.
    (He goes over to **TRIGGER***.)*
TRIGGER. Oh, cripes on a bike.
AARVID. Lovely. Okay, are ya ready for your question?
TRIGGER. Is that my question?
AARVID. No. Okay, here's your question…
    (reading from a card)
    Who is buried in Grant's tomb?
TRIGGER. *(thinks)* Can I phone a friend?
AARVID. No, you can't. Grant's Tomb. Who is buried in Grant's Tomb?

TRIGGER. *(thinks)* I would wish for peace on earth. My own apartment. And for global warming.

(**AARVID** *leans over and whispers something to* **TRIGGER**. **TRIGGER** *looks at the camera.*)

TRIGGER. *(cont.)* For no global warming…Cause it's bad.

(to **AARVID** *)*

How 'bout just February? It's really cold.

KANUTE. *(looking out the window)* Hey, it looks like Gunner is pullin' in, there.

TRIGGER. Oh, crap, well, let me know when he's gone.

(She exits to the bathroom.)

AARVID. Oh, I think you'll know…Alright, let's go to Bernice.

(He goes over to her.)

Ya look so beautiful, there.

BERNICE. Thank you. I made my fishnet stockings out of fish nets.

(We hear a rim-shot from the karaoke machine. To the machine.)

That's not a joke.

AARVID. So talented. Okay, here's your question.

(He reads from a card.)

If you could marry anyone in the world, who would it be?

BERNICE. Kanute.

KANUTE. *(excited)* Really?!

BERNICE. *(proud of her joke)* Sarcasm!

AARVID. *(He laughs.)* Oh, that's funny…She would marry me.

(to **BERNICE**, *smiling)*

Wouldn't ya.

(**BERNICE** *ignores him, looking straight ahead, then turns and goes into the kitchen.*)

KANUTE. *(into mic)* Awkward.

AARVID. Okay, let's go to Clara. Ya ready?

> (**GUNNER** *enters the bar and sees* **CLARA** *for the first time in her evening gown. She's beautiful.*)

CLARA. Yah, okay, go ahead.

AARVID. Alright, here's your question...

> *(reading from the card)*

Name the first ten presidents.

CLARA. *(a little perturbed at her difficult question, then quickly rattles them off)* George Washington, John Adams, Thomas Jefferson, James Madison, James Monroe, John Quincy Adams, Andrew Jackson, Martin Van Buren, William Harrison and Tippy Canoe and John Tyler, too.

> *(pleased with herself)*

AARVID. *(looks at card)* You gotta be kiddin' me?

CLARA. Should I keep goin'?

> (**GUNNER** *laughs. He writes something on a piece of paper.* **CLARA** *turns and looks at him.*)

Oh, hey, Gunner.

GUNNER. *(stares at her, mesmerized by her beauty)* Hey.

CLARA. *(after an awkward moment)* Ya wanna stay and watch?

GUNNER. What? No. I just...brought in some more scores.

> (*He holds the piece of paper out, while continuing to stare at her.* **AARVID** *takes it from him.* **CLARA** *smiles.*)

AARVID. *(comparing* **GUNNER**'s *scores with* **KANUTE**'s *scores)* Okay, let's see what we got, here. There was a three way tie in the "pontoon wear" event. Which means someone voted for Trigger.

> *(He shoots a look at* **KANUTE**.*)*

KANUTE. *(while flipping a "2" under* **BERNICE**'s *and* **CLARA**'s *name and a "3" under* **TRIGGER**'s *name)* Coulda been Hasselhoff. I hear he likes big women.

AARVID. Bernice won the evening gown event...

> *(yelling to the kitchen)*

Love you!

BERNICE. *(offstage) (from the kitchen)* Whatever!

(KANUTE flips a "3" under BERNICE's name.)

AARVID. *(looking at the scores)* There was a three way tie in the "Bait the hook" event.

(looking at KANUTE)

Even with Trigger's "dynamite"…

(Before KANUTE can speak, AARVID cuts him off. KANUTE flips a "3" under CLARA's name and a "4" under TRIGGER's and BERNICE's name.)

…and Clara won the final question…

(KANUTE flips a "4" under CLARA's name. AARVID hands CLARA a blue ribbon.)

CLARA. Oh, my gosh. Wow!

AARVID. So there's a three-way tie goin' into the last event.

(looking at KANUTE)

Hard to believe it's even close.

KANUTE. *(into mic)* Hasselhoff…

AARVID. …Okay, our final event is…oh, wait, we need Trigger.

GUNNER. Oh, crap.

(GUNNER quickly exits the bar.)

CLARA. I'll go check on her.

(She goes in to the bathroom.)

Everything okay in there, Trigger?

TRIGGER. *(offstage)* Yah, everything is just fine. Is Gunner still out there?

CLARA. *(Offstage)* No, he's gone.

AARVID. We need Bernice, too.

(yelling to the kitchen)

Bernice!

BERNICE. *(Offstage)* Just a minute!

AARVID. *(to the camera)* While we're waitin' for my little lambchop, how 'bout another word from our sponsor.

(KANUTE blows into a pitch pipe. AARVID accompanies KANUTE's hip hop, rap number by "scratching" into the mic.)

KANUTE.
KANUTE'S ICE HOLE,
KANUTE'S ICE HOLE AUGER,
IT'LL MAKE YOU'RE AUGERIN' EASIER.
ICE HOLE AUGERIN' EASIER,
EASIER, EASIER, EASIER.
ICE HOLE AUGERIN' EASIER.

KANUTE & AARVID.
ICE HOLE!

AARVID. Ya know, Kanute, when I think of ice holes, I totally think of you.

KANUTE. Thank you.

AARVID. Okay, our final event is "Talent." Can we get everyone out here, please!

(CLARA and TRIGGER come out of the bathroom. BERNICE comes out of the kitchen wearing a robe.)

There she is. Are ya ready, my sweetness?

BERNICE. Yah.

(The music starts. BERNICE drops her robe. Underneath is a sexy patriotic outfit.)

AARVID. Holy moly.

BERNICE. *(sings)*
I'M A BUNYAN WOMAN.
A BUNYAN WOMAN THRU AND THRU.
YOU MAY BE ABLE TO LEAVE BUNYAN BAY,
BUT THE BUNYAN STAYS IN YOU.

THERE'S A FAIR IN BUNYAN COUNTY,
YOU CAN RIDE A PONY.
THEY HAVE LUNCH MEAT ON A STICK
THEY CALL IT FRIED BALONEY.

BEAUTIFUL FOR SPACIOUS SKIES,
I LOVE MY BUNYAN BAY.

BERNICE. *(cont.)*
WHERE YOU CAN GET YOUR CAMPING GEAR
ON SALE THRU LABOR DAY.

OH, I'M GLAD I LIVE IN THE LAND OF BUNYAN,
MAKES ME CRY LIKE A DICED UP ONION.
LOOK AWAY, LOOK AWAY, LOOK AWAY, BUNYAN LAND.

MY HOME WILL REMAIN BUNYAN COUNTY.
THERE IS NO PLACE THAT I WOULD RATHER BE.
WHERE BRAVE SOLDIERS GO TO THE BUNYAN,
WHERE ON WEDNESDAY THEY HAVE BUY ONE GET ONE
FREE.

BUNYAN BAY. LOTS TO DO, LOTS TO SEE, BUNYAN BAY.
BUY A SOUVENIR, YOU CAN EAT SOME DEER,
AT THE SWEDISH ALL-YOU-EAT BUFFET.

THERE'S KANUTE'S DEER PETTING FARM,
WHERE YA RIDE A DRUGGED UP MOOSE.
MAKE US YOUR FINAL DESTINATION.

I'M A BUNYAN WOMAN,
A BUNYAN WOMAN THRU AND THRU.
YOU MAY BE ABLE TO LEAVE BUNYAN BAY,
BUT THE BUNYAN STAYS IN YOU.

AARVID. *(into mic, getting lost in his thoughts)* That was wonderful, Bernice. I am so in love with you. So in love with you. I think of you day and night, night and day, with every fiber of my being…

KANUTE. *(into mic)* …Still on the air.

AARVID. *(catches himself)* Be professional, be professional.

(to the camera)

Okay, next up in the talent event is Trigger.

TRIGGER. Gin dangit.

AARVID. I can hardly wait to hear what you'll be doing tonight.

TRIGGER. *(Taking the mic from* **AARVID**. *Into mic.)* Tonight I will be performing the written word.

KANUTE. *(whispers into mic)* The written word.

AARVID. A little culture in the competition.

TRIGGER. That's right, Aarvid. I will be reciting a poem, while cracking a walnut with my butt cheeks.

KANUTE. *(whispering into mic)* Butt cheeks.

*(**AARVID** leans over and whispers something to **TRIGGER**.)*

TRIGGER. There will be no walnut…

*(to **AARVID**, whispering)*

But it's already in there. Should I take it out?

*(**AARVID** shakes his head and mouths "no.")*

I wrote this during a cigar break at work.

(very dramatic)

A car drove by,
the headlights flash-id,
the break pads squeal-id,
a squirrel got smash-id.

(End of poem. She contorts her body and grimaces. We hear a walnut cracking.)

I didn't think that would hurt so much.

AARVID. So glad I'm hosting this.

KANUTE. It's hard to find a good nutcracker.

TRIGGER. I think I need a big wet kiss.

*(She holds her arms out, lips puckered, and goes to kiss **KANUTE**. The phone rings.)*

KANUTE. Telephone!

*(**KANUTE** quickly answers it, avoiding the kiss.)*

The Bunyan…

*(He looks at **TRIGGER**.)*

Yes, officer…uh huh…uh huh…really?…Wow!… No, I will not let on. My lips are sealed… Okey dokey… You betcha.

(He hangs up.)

That was the Bunyan Bay police. They're on their way to pick up Trigger.

CLARA & BERNICE & AARVID. What?!

KANUTE. Apparently, she's wanted for impersonating a forest ranger. I guess that's a felony or somethin'.

CLARA & BERNICE & AARVID. Trigger!

TRIGGER. That is not true. I *am* a forest ranger.

(looks at her watch)

Oh my gosh, would ya look at the time, there. I gotta go and…forest range.

(She heads for the door.)

KANUTE. Ya know, I think they wanted ya to stay.

TRIGGER. *(turns back)* Oh, yah, I'd love to stay but I'm really late. Honey, we might have to postpone the wedding.

KANUTE. *(insincere)* Darn it.

AARVID. What about Miss Walleye Queen?

TRIGGER. I hereby withdraw my candidacy. Good luck, girls.

*(to **KANUTE**)*

We'll talk.

(She opens the door and looks out.)

Oh, crap, it's Gunner. He's here.

(She exits.)

You squealed on me, didn't ya?!

*(While outside, **TRIGGER** "changes into **GUNNER**." On the score board, **AARVID** flips **TRIGGER**'s score from "4" to "0.")*

GUNNER. *(offstage)* Ya can't tell people you're a forest ranger!

TRIGGER. *(offstage)* I work *near* the forest!

GUNNER. *(offstage)* Ya remove road kill from highways!

TRIGGER. *(offstage)* They are life challenged!

GUNNER. *(offstage)* Hit the bricks, ya mouth breather!

TRIGGER. *(offstage)* I am so outta here!

GUNNER. *(offstage)* Good!

*(**GUNNER** enters the bar. Everyone looks at him.)*

Hey.

EVERYONE. *(Ad lib)* Hey, Gunner. How's it goin'? *(Etc.)*

*(**GUNNER** steps down to get closer to **CLARA**. She's beautiful in her evening gown. **GUNNER** just stares at her, amazed at her beauty. **CLARA** blushes.)*

AARVID. So, Kanute, I guess ya learned a pretty valuable lesson, there.

KANUTE. Nope.

AARVID. Okay…

*(looking at **GUNNER**)*

Alright, since Gunner is here let's go ahead and announce the winner of the fishin' contest and then we'll do Clara's final talent event.

(He opens up an envelope.)

I'll just open the sealed envelope, here.

(He pulls out a piece of paper, and looks at it.)

Let's see here. Martha Stordahl caught a four ounce perch. That's more like catchin' bait, huh, fellas? Lars Yensen caught a 12 ounce crappie. Harold Lundeen caught a one and a half pound blue gill, and…oh, here, Gunner Johnson caught a walleye weighin' two pounds, four ounces. Not bad, there, big guy.

GUNNER. Yah, okay, what did Kanute get?

AARVID. *(looking at the paper)* Kanute. Okay, let's see here… Oh, here. Kanute caught a walleye that weighed…

(We hear a drum roll from the karaoke machine.)

Upgrade.

GUNNER. Oh, would ya just tell us!

(The drum roll stops.)

AARVID. *(looking at paper)* Three pounds, 2 ounces.

GUNNER. Crap!

KANUTE. Yes! Yes!

(dancing around the bar)

I win! The bar is mine! Mine, mine, mine, mine, mine…

(He kisses the bar.)

BERNICE. …Kanute.

GUNNER. *(to* **CLARA***)* I'm sorry. I just…I thought I won for sure. I really did…

*(***CLARA***, upset, looks away.)*

Oh, come on, Clara, I'm sorry, okay. We'll get the bar back, we will. I'll figure somethin' out, okay. I promise. I'll get it back. I'm just…I'm really sorry.

AARVID. Congratulations, Kanute, and the winner of the Bunyan County Fair fishin' contest is Clara Johnson.

GUNNER & KANUTE. What?

CLARA. I won?

AARVID. Clara entered, didn't know that, and caught a wall-eye weighin' four pounds, five ounces.

CLARA. It was four pounds?

KANUTE. That's a kick in the Johnsonville.

CLARA. *(mimicking* **KANUTE***)* Store number two is mine! Mine, mine, mine, mine, mine…

KANUTE. …Hey! No, okay, cause the bet was with Gunner, not you.

CLARA. I own half the bar, so the bet was with me too.

KANUTE. I was only bettin' for *Gunner's* half.

CLARA. Yah, right, well, don't worry about it, Kanute, I don't want your stupid store, anyway.

KANUTE. Sweet.

CLARA. I tell ya what, just pay your bar tab and we'll call it even.

KANUTE. *(not liking the sound of that)* Ahhhh…

AARVID. …And here is your five hundred dollars.

(He hands **CLARA** *a check.)*

Congratulations!

(AARVID and BERNICE applaud.)

CLARA. Thanks.

BERNICE. Alright, Clara!

CLARA & BERNICE. *(putting their hands on their heads like Viking horns, mimicking KANUTE and GUNNER's "Code of the Norse" yell.)* Aaahoooo!

GUNNER. So…you went fishin' today?

CLARA. Yah, I went trollin' out at Mosquito Point for a half hour durin' lunch.

GUNNER. So…ya didn't think I could do it?

CLARA. No, it's not that, it's just that, ya know…insurance.

AARVID. What kinda bait did ya use?

CLARA. A Daredevil with Spam.

(The music starts.)

AARVID & KANUTE & BERNICE.
SHE CAUGHT THE FISH WITH SPAM,
SHE CAUGHT THE FISH WITH SPAM…

GUNNER. *(to the karaoke machine)* …Oh, come on! Seriously!

(The machine stops. Quietly angry, to CLARA.)

You used…Spam to win the fishin' contest?

CLARA. *(sarcastic)* Yaaay! We saved the bar! Yaaay!

GUNNER. *(despondent)* I don't know what to say…I mean, everyone in town knows that I bet the bar, thanks for announcin' it. And sure it may not have been the best decision I ever made, okay, maybe even the worst decision, alright, but I did it to try and impress you, okay. Ya know, win the contest and win Kanute's store so I could afford to buy ya stuff, ya know, like a man is supposed to do for his wife, okay. And what do ya do? Ya come thru again, like ya always do. Ya saved the bar, and for the rest of my life I will be known as the guy who's wife saved him with Spam.

(The music starts. Quickly, to the machine.)

Don't even think about it!

(It stops.)

CLARA. I'm sorry, okay. I was just thinkin' maybe it was a good thing I caught the fish so we didn't lose the bar.

GUNNER. Yah, well, now everyone knows who wears the pants in this family.

CLARA. I did it for us.

GUNNER. Yah, just like puttin' yourself on tv and paradin' around in your little Walleye Queen outfit, is for *us*.

CLARA. I just wanted ya to notice me.

GUNNER. Yah, well, the whole town is noticin' ya now. Congratulations. I hope you're happy.

(He exits to the kitchen. After a few beats of silence.)

AARVID. *(trying to lighten up a very awkward situation)* Okay, umm, we have one more event, here, and that would be Clara's talent, and, ahh…

(He looks at **CLARA**. *She's very sad.)*

You don't have to do this if ya don't want to.

CLARA. No, I'm fine. I'll do it.

(She takes the microphone from **AARVID**.*)*

Umm…I had somethin' I picked out to sing, but I don't really feel like doin' that one right now, so I'm gonna do somethin' else.

(to the karaoke machine)

"Bunyan Bay."

(The music starts.)

(sings into mic)

THERE IS A PLACE I'LL ALWAYS LOVE,
A PLACE I'M ALWAYS THINKING OF
WHENEVER LIFE HAS TAKEN ME AWAY.
WHERE FRIENDS AND FAMILY WELCOME ME,
A PLACE MY HEART WILL ALWAYS BE,
I WISH I DIDN'T HAVE TO LEAVE TODAY.
BUNYAN BAY.

BERNICE & KANUTE & AARVID.

BUNYAN BAY.

(CLARA smiles endearing to them.)

CLARA.

HOW I HATE TO LEAVE MY FRIENDS IN BUNYAN BAY.

BERNICE & KANUTE & AARVID.

BUNYAN BAY.

CLARA.

WHERE THE NORTHERN LIGHTS ARE BRIGHT,
AND THE LOONS SING OUT AT NIGHT.
IT'S A PLACE THAT I WILL ALWAYS CALL MY HOME.

I WANTED SO TO SHARE HIS LIFE,
I TRIED MY BEST TO BE HIS WIFE,
BUT NOW I KNOW IT'S BEST THAT WE'RE APART.
THE TIME HAS COME FOR ME TO LEAVE,
I NEED SOME TIME FOR ME TO GRIEVE,
THE LOSS THAT GAVE TO ME A BROKEN HEART.
BUNYAN BAY.

(GUNNER comes out of the kitchen. CLARA doesn't see him. He places some scores on the bar.)

BERNICE & KANUTE & AARVID.

BUNYAN BAY.

CLARA.

I WILL MISS MY LIFE MY HOME IN BUNYAN BAY.

BERNICE & KANUTE & AARVID.

BUNYAN BAY.

CLARA.

I'M AFRAID I HAVE TO SAY,
THAT I HAVE TO LEAVE TODAY.
IF MY HEART WILL EVER HEAL,
I'LL COME BACK HOME.

(emotional)

I'm sorry.

(In tears, CLARA turns away from GUNNER and heads toward the bathroom. GUNNER grabs the other mic. Just as she's about to exit, she hears GUNNER sing and stops. During the song, she slowly turns to GUNNER, making him work for it.)

GUNNER. *(sings into mic)*
> THERE ARE THREE WORDS I NEED TO SAY,
> THREE WORDS THAT SEEM TO SLIP AWAY,
> I KNOW THAT I SHOULD SAY THEM MORE THAN ONCE.
> TO SOMEONE SPECIAL ALL AGREE,
> UNTIL NOW SHE PUT UP WITH ME.
> A GUY WHEN TRYIN' TO SAY THOSE WORDS, HE GRUNTS.
> I LLL HER. *(He can't say "I love you.")*

BERNICE & KANUTE & AARVID.
> HE LLL'S HER.

GUNNER.
> I AM SORRY THAT I DID THE THINGS THAT HURT HER.

BERNICE & KANUTE & AARVID.
> REALLY HURT HER.

GUNNER.
> SHE MEANS EVERYTHING TO ME.
> I WISH I COULD LET HER SEE.
> I CAN SAY THE WORDS THAT I SAID ONCE BEFORE.
> I LLL-URV HER. *(He still can't say it.)*

BERNICE & KANUTE & AARVID.
> HE LLL-URVS HER.

GUNNER.
> HOW MY LIFE WILL NEVER BE COMPLETE WITHOUT HER.

BERNICE & KANUTE & AARVID.
> CAUSE HE LLL-URVS HER.

GUNNER.
> IF SHE'LL JUST COME BACK TO ME,
> I WILL PROVE TO HER YOU'LL SEE,
> THAT SHE'LL KNOW HOW MUCH I CARE FOR HER EACH DAY.
> I LOVE YOU.

BERNICE & KANUTE & AARVID.
> HOLY CRAP.

GUNNER.
> EVERY NEW DAY I WILL LOVE YOU MORE THAN EVER.

BERNICE & KANUTE & AARVID.
> HOLY CRAP.

GUNNER.
  IF YOU JUST COME BACK TO ME,
GUNNER & CLARA.
  THIS TO YOU I GUARANTEE,
  ALL MY LOVE I'LL GIVE TO YOU FOREVERMORE.
  (They kiss.)

BERNICE. Oh, I think I'm gonna cry.

KANUTE. I think I threw up in my mouth a little.

  *(**KANUTE** and **AARVID** quietly confer, looking at **KANUTE**'s clip board along with **GUNNER**'s scores.)*

GUNNER. I'm sorry I was such a butt head, Clara. Ya mean everything to me, and…I really do love you.

CLARA. *(playful)* Oh, I love you too, Gunner…Ya butt head.

GUNNER. Ya know, by the way, you are beautiful.

CLARA. No.

GUNNER. I'm serious. I mean, you're glamorous like a movie star. Like Adrienne Barbeau.

CLARA. Oh, stop it.

GUNNER. Okay, I'll stop.

CLARA. No, keep goin'.

GUNNER. You are. You're a looker. And I'm not just sayin' that cause ya saved my butt, okay. I mean, you are a babe. Seriously. Look at her. Wow.

KANUTE. *(looking over to her)* Oh, yah, I am lookin'. You betcha. Up and down, left and right. And me likey. Hubba hubba, ah-ooga ah-ooga,

  (like he's looking thru a submarine periscope)

  dive, dive, dive…

  *(turning to **GUNNER** who shoots **KANUTE** a look)*

  Too much?

GUNNER. Yah.

AARVID. *(looking at a piece of paper)* Okay, we have the final results here…And the winner of the Bunyan County Fair Miss Walleye Queen competition is…Clara Johnson.

CLARA. What?!

GUNNER. *(pleasantly surprised)* What?

KANUTE. What?

BERNICE. *(upset)* What?!

> *(to* **KANUTE** *and* **AARVID** *)*
>
> Okay, which one of you two voted for Clara?!

AARVID & KANUTE. *(busted, at a loss for words)* Aaaaaaaaah…

BERNICE. …Both of you!?

AARVID. It was a very sad song.

KANUTE. *(Sheepish. Holds out a cracked walnut, offering it to* **BERNICE***.)* Ya wanna Walnut?

EVERYONE. *(gross)* Ohh!

> *(He pops it in his mouth. An even bigger groan.)*
>
> OHH!
>
> *(***AARVID** *goes to put the crown on* **CLARA***'s head and hands her flowers.)*

AARVID. Here ya go, Clara…

CLARA. …Yah, umm…

> *(holding off* **AARVID** *on the crown)*
>
> Thanks and everything but I'm afraid I'm disqualified.

AARVID. Why?

CLARA. Cause I'm married.

> *(***GUNNER** *puts his arm around* **CLARA***.)*

AARVID. Yah, I know, but ya can be married as long as the relationship is in a turbulent pla…

> *(realizes)*
>
> Oh, yah, I get it. It's not turbulent anymore. See, I'm followin' this. Which means the new Miss Walleye Queen is Bernice Lundstrom.
>
> *(***AARVID** *puts the crown on* **BERNICE** *and hands her flowers.)*

(On the score board, **KANUTE** *flips* **CLARA**'s *score from "4" to "0," then goes over to* **BERNICE**. **GUNNER** *and* **CLARA** *go behind the bar, they lower the block of butter down below the bar and start "carving" the block of butter.)*

BERNICE. *(ecstatic)* Oh, my gosh. Oh, my gosh. This is the greatest thing that's ever happened to me in my life. It's so unexpected.

KANUTE. You were the only one left.

BERNICE. I just wanna thank Bunyan Bay for givin' me this opportunity...

KANUTE. ...There were no other options.

BERNICE. I wanna thank all the other contestants...

KANUTE. ...You were the only contestant.

BERNICE. Kanute, do you *ever* wanna have a chance with me again?

KANUTE. Super job! I was rootin' for ya.

AARVID. So, Bernice, did you, ahh, make a decision yet on, ya know, marryin' me?

BERNICE. Ya know, Aarvid, I was thinkin' about it...but then Kanute pointed out in the pamphlet, that the Walleye Queen can't get engaged for a year.

AARVID. It doesn't say that.

KANUTE. *(holding pamphlet in front of* **AARVID***)* They accepted my addendum.

AARVID. I hate you.

KANUTE. *(raising his arms above his head)* Still in the game!

BERNICE. *(to* **CLARA***)* Thanks for lettin' me win, honey.

CLARA. *(putting the "Miss Walleye Queen" sash on* **BERNICE***)* You deserve it.

(They hug.)

KANUTE. Okay, then, let's welcome the new Miss Walleye Queen, who will not be gettin' engaged to Aarvid for a year.

AARVID. Or Kanute.

(The music starts. **BERNICE** *walks around the stage waving to the audience.)*

KANUTE. *(sings)*
HERE'S OUR BEAUTIFUL QUEEN
NO FINER EVER SEEN
NO CHALLENGER, SO SHE WON FIRST PLACE,
SHE'S OUR WALLEYE QUEEN, SOON A BUTTER FACE.

AARVID.
WATCH HER ON THE BIG SCREEN,
OUR CORN FED BEAUTY QUEEN.
OH, SHE'S ALL DAIRY, CAN WORK A PLOW,
NOT A FAKE.

KANUTE & GUNNER & CLARA & AARVID.
SHE COMES FROM THE COW.

*(***BERNICE*** *reacts.)*

(While **KANUTE** *and* **AARVID** *sing,* **GUNNER** *brings out the finished sculpture of* **BERNICE***'s face carved in butter. There's a towel over it.)*

KANUTE.
SHE'S OUR BUTTER FACE QUEEN,
NO FAT FREE MARGER-EEN.
SHE'S NOT A STICK, NOT A BUTTER PAT,
SHE'S A BIG 'OL BLOCK OF SATURATED FAT.

*(***CLARA*** *removes the towel, presenting the butter face.* **BERNICE** *reacts. She takes the butter face from* **GUNNER** *and parades it around the stage.)*

AARVID.
HERE'S OUR BEAUTIFUL QUEEN,
OUR BUTTER FIGURINE.

KANUTE.
THE REAL THING, NOT A SUBSTITUTE,

AARVID.
SHE LOOKS SO DARN GOOD IN A SWIMMING SUIT,

KANUTE.
SHE IS CARVED IN BUTTER CAUSE

KANUTE & GUNNER & CLARA & AARVID.
SHE'S OUR WALLEYE QUEEN!

(As soon as the song ends, the next song begins. **KANUTE** *takes the butter face from* **BERNICE** *and puts it on the bar, then comes back and joins the rest in singing.)*

EVERYONE. *(singing)*
FIRST YA STAND LIKE A FROZEN DEER IN THE HEADLIGHTS.
THEN YA SPIN LIKE A TWISTER IN JUNE.
HANDS UP HIGH,
THEN YA SWING YOUR THIGHS,
JUST LIKE YA WOULD ON A SINKING PONTOON.
THEN GET HAPPY FEET, LIKE A MOOSE IN HEAT,
AND FLAP YOUR ARMS LIKE YA SAW A WILD BOAR.
THEN YA JUMP UP STRAIGHT, IN A GOPHER STATE,
AND SHAKE YOUR FINS LIKE A FISH ON THE FLOOR.
SHAKE YOUR FINS!

End of Play

PROPERTIES LIST

ACT I

Onstage:
>Furniture:
>2 tables (30 – 36 inch diameter) (stage right, stage left)
>4 chairs without arm rests (right and left of each table)
>Bar (6-8 feet depending on size of set)
>2-3 bar stools

Props and Dressing:

On Tables:
>2 restaurant napkin holders with napkins
>2 sets of salt and pepper shakers
>4 food menus (2 on each table)

On Bar:
>Deck of cards on bar dealt out for Gunner & Kanute's Gin game
>2 Beer mugs filled ½ way for Gunner & Kanute
>A fishing magazine
>Telephone

On Floor
>Extremely large karaoke machine (see sample drawing)
>2 Wireless microphones (on top of karaoke machine)
>2 Karaoke song menus (on top of karaoke machine)
>Remote control for karaoke machine (on top of karaoke machine)

On Walls:
>Beer signs
>Stuffed fish and various other stuffed animals
>Sign that reads, "Bunyan County Fair Fishing Contest - Grand Prize $500 - Register Here."
>2 fishing poles. Used for the song, "Who's Better Catching Fish."
>Five coat hooks for purse, fox hat, etc. (by front door)

Underneath bar:
>4 beer mugs
>2 bar towels
>Serving tray

Behind bar:
    Liquor bottles
    Sports trophies
    Beer tower
    Beer (preferably non-alcoholic)

Props for "Bunyan County Has the Best Fair" (NOTE: These props are optional. If they can be acquired, they make the production more fun. The song, "Bunyan County Has the Best Fair" has also been done using a slide show during the song with funny county fair photos. see photos on www.adonthugmecountyfair. com.):
    A water bottle
    A tree branch
    Several pair of women's underwear
    Hay
    A poster on foam board of:
                - a cow
                - a train
                - a walleye
                - an antelope
                - a roller coaster
                - a piece of pie on a stick
                - a "Tunnel of Like"

KANUTE carries with him:
    A ring box holding a large engagement ring

CLARA brings in:
    Brown paper bag with groceries

GUNNER brings in:
    7 greeting cards for the song, "When Ya Need to Share Your Feelings, Get a Card."

AARVID brings in:
    - He wears a "fox hat" when he enters (see photo on www.adonthugmecountyfair.com)
    - He carries a pamphlet, "bylaws" for the Walleye Queen Competition.

AARVID carries with him for the song "I'm the Man You'll Marry":
    A ring box holding a small ring.

Other props:
Rap gear, "bling," that **KANUTE, AARVID** and **BERNICE**
put on for the song, "What Did Gunner Do?"

ACT II

In Kitchen:
-Bernice's face carved in butter on a platter. This comes out
at the end of the play.

On top of Bar:
A Scoreboard on top of the bar with Clara, Bernice and Trigger's names across the bottom, and numbers above their
names that can be flipped over when they win an event. It
starts at "0" under each of their names, and goes up to "4"
during the contest. See photo on website.
Walnuts in a bowl

Under/Behind Bar:
A block of butter (fake) on a platter. See photo on website.
Trigger's "Roadkill Squirrel" art for the Taxidermy event –
can be placed before ACT I
Clara's "Seed slash Vegetable art "Wishful Thinking" – can
be placed before ACT I
3 plain "bare" hooks for Trigger, Clara, and Bernice's "Bait
the Hook" event
3 "baited" hooks for the "Bait the Hook" event
  - Trigger's baited hook will be a stick of dynamite
  (preferably not real).
  - Bernice's baited hook will be a small fake minnow
  on a hook.
  - Clara's baited hook will be a huge tackle with several hooks. On each hook are fake minnows, worms,
  and other types of bait. It's truly a work of art.

Other Props:
A pitch pipe for Kanute
Envelope with the results of the fishing contest
Index cards with scores on them
A clipboard
3 Blue ribbons; one for the "Seed slash Vegetable Art," one
for "Roadkill Squirrel," and one that Aarvid hands to Clara.
Mr. Potato Head with real potato and a Red ribbon on it that
Bernice brings out

A tiara, for the winner of the Walleye Queen Competition
Fake roses for the winner of the Walleye Queen Competition
4 sashes; one with Clara's name, Trigger's name, and Bernice's name, and a fourth with "Miss Walleye Queen," on it.

Costumes:

The three ladies will need outfits for the "Pontoon Wear" event, and the "Evening Gown" event. Trigger will need a wig, glasses, and dresses with bras sewn in, that can be put on and taken off quickly for Gunner/Trigger's quick changes.
A "Miss Firecracker" outfit for Bernice (see photo on website) The Miss Firecracker outfit that Bernice wears can be purchased online.

Please visit www.adonthugmecountyfair.com to see photos of the props as well as photos of the set.

The posters can be created from online stock photo sources or purchased from several sources including Ebay, Amazon.com, online poster stores, etc.

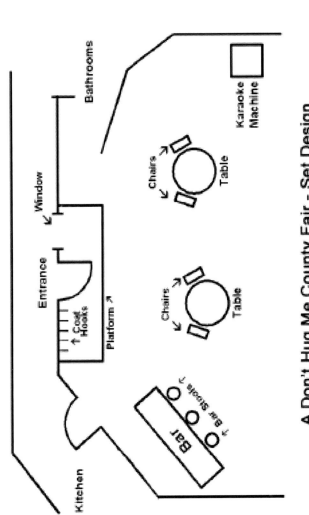

A Don't Hug Me County Fair - Set Design
(for photos of the set from the Los Angeles production, visit:
www.adonthugmecountyfair.com)

Not quite to scale - but close enough

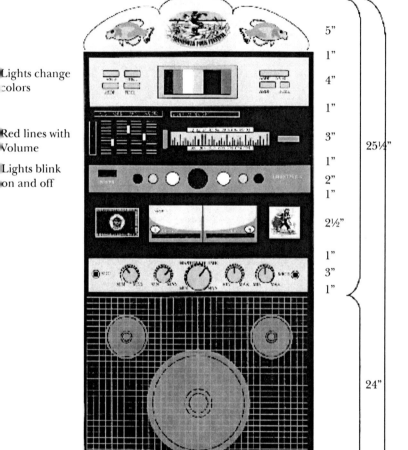

Lights change
colors

Red lines with
Volume

Lights blink
on and off

5"

1"

4"

1"

3"

1"

2"

1"

2½"

1"

3"

1"

25¼"

24"

Life Style G50

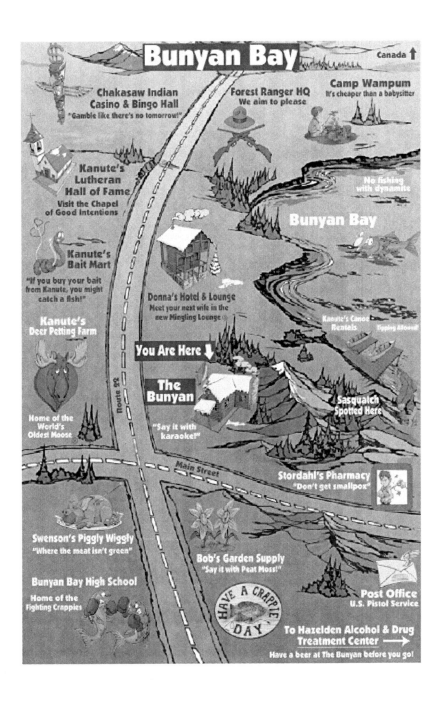

From the reviews of
A Don't Hug Me County Fair...

"It's wonderful!" -
– Dick Clark, TV Icon

"Riotously funny!"
– *Norwegian American Weekly*

"A fun romp that is bound to be a popular superhit! RECOMMENDED!"
-- *Grigware Talks Theatre*

"I laughed so hard, my sides hurt!"
– *American Radio Network*

"Thigh slapping fun!...Go see it!"
– *LA TACO*

"I love to laugh, and I did!...It is just the sort of play that an earnest, energetic
small theatre company would love to mount!"
– *LATheatreReview.com*

"GO!...Crowd pleasing!"
– *LA WEEKLY*

"Phil Olson's jokes are as frequent as mosquito bites. They just keep
coming…I laughed so hard and so often that I might have damaged some of
my sturdy Norwegian innards!"
– *LA Comedy Examiner*

"100% Sweet!"
– *Bitter-Lemons.com*

"A howl-a-minute hoot!...Following the success of *Don't Hug Me* and *A
Don't Hug Me Christmas Carol*, which both tour the U.S., this is the third in
the series. In my opinion, this is the most outrageously zany and riotously
entertaining of the trio!"
– *Tolucan Times*

"This extremely funny and charming musical has more genuine laughs per min-
ute than any recently staged comedy presented within the Los Angeles area!...
This stage production is part of the *Don't Hug Me* series, written by Phil Olson.
However, this specific musical stands out on its own! That is, if you never saw
Don't Hug Me, don't worry, you won't be left in the dark at all!"
– *Accessibly Live*

"You won't want to miss the fun of this third trip to Bunyan Bay!"
- *Stage Happenings*

Breinigsville, PA USA
20 November 2009
227953BV00004B/3/P